The Murders on Cayo Costa

The Murders on Cayo Costa

Elia Chepaitis

The Murders on Cayo Costa is a work of fiction. Any resemblance to persons living or dead, or to actual events, is unintended and accidental, but the island itself and the park's features are authentic. The author attempted to describe locations and activities on Cayo Costa as accurately as possible, hoping that readers will visit and enjoy this magical and well-managed treasure.

This novel is a murder mystery, a romance, and an adventure story— best read during an island vacation, real or imaginary. The author wishes to thank Cayo Costa's park rangers and staff for their unfailing kindness, encouragement, and assistance. Many thanks also to the Key West Writers Guild for their fellowship, advice, and commitment to the art; to PaddleFlorida, Inc. for their expertise, well-organized expeditions, and dedication to enlightened water management; to fellow campers and kayakers for their feedback and comradery; to a far-flung tribe of diligent and thoughtful readers for their insights and suggestions; and to Joe and Amy Chepaitis for their understanding and love.

Photography and graphics by Elia Chepaitis

ISBN-13: 9781546928218
ISBN-10: 1546928219

Also by the author:

Fiction:

Murder with Kayaks in the Florida Keys
Poppy Tears: A Victorian Mystery [forthcoming: excerpt included]

For children:

Pete the Incredible Puffer Fish: A Love Story in the Florida Keys

History:

The Opium of the Children: Domestic Opium and Child Drugging in Early
Victorian England [dissertation, on Library of Congress microfiche]

In memory of my creative and adventuresome brothers
Lou, Jack, and Bill

Cayo Costa Cabins

Beach Path   Beach Path

ʌ   ʌ
| |

←tents

←pavilion   Cabin 7

                                                        seashore

                                                        Oscar, Ted +

                                                        Sally Coleman

        M/F

     restroom

=============================ROAD============================

Cabin 1	Cabin 2	Cabin 3	Cabin 4	Cabin 5	Cabin 6
sea oat	*sea grape*	*sea horse*	*sea breeze*	*sea fan*	*sea turtle*
Philip Schwartz	Spencer Clark+	Detective Gabriel	Melony+	Olivia	Will+
Morgan +	Mary Ellison	Ortillo, Deputies	Keisha	Longo	Mason
Sebby		Margery Christie			
		+ Adrian Fitzhugh			

=======================ROAD===========================

Cabin 8	F/M	Cabin 9	Cabin 10	Cabin 11	M/F	Cabin 12
sea lavender	restroom	*sea shell*	*sea view*	*sea shore*	restroom	*sea star*
Gilbert		Fred		Boris, Tamara,		Libera
Newsome		Kenichi		Paul, Sasha +Stas		Grimaldi
				Rodzianko		

Prologue

The landing at Cayo Costa was silent and still. No ferries were moored at the pier and no children dangled crab nets from the wharves, even though it was low tide. Every tram and kayak was idle, and there was not a fisherman, shell seeker, bicyclist, or sun lover in sight. All of them were at the pavilion near the beach path, waiting to be questioned again.

On Monday, a body had turned up at the landing, or, more accurately, floated up. And, as if that weren't enough, early that morning, another camper had been attacked and might not survive. And it was only Tuesday.

Deputy Margery Christie edged out of Ranger Edward's office and paused at the top of the stairs. Her boss, Detective Inspector Gabriel Ortillo was draped across the passenger seat in the staff cart below, still absorbed in that cabin chart, she noticed. She stole past him, barely glancing at his Mestizo-handsome face, the long lashes, the sharp cheekbones. When did he shave on these round-the-clock assignments? She had never seen him with stubble.

He didn't lift his head. She knew that look—serene and beatific, in another world and perhaps not an altogether nice one. Murder animated him. Sometimes his intensity freaked her out.

Gabriel studied the chart, riveted, reviewing the occupants, slightly twitching his right foot. What was going on in those cabins? As baffling and horrific as the crimes were, he would be the first to admit that he loved the mess of it all, especially that first shock. He was born for this. When he heard the helicopter in the distance, returning with the arson team, he reluctantly slid out of the seat.

He was ready. Today we sort this out, catch up, catch up to him—this ruthless killer who strikes with such confidence and impunity. What's the logic behind these artful, swift, premeditated attacks? What is he doing here in the middle of nowhere, and what the hell is driving him? Who is he after?

Leaning over the front bumper, Gabe slowly smoothed the chart again and ran a finger from one cabin to another. The answer was here; they had to find a motive. Without any leads and no suspect, they had to learn more about these campers. One might be the next victim, or possibly a murderer. Did these people know each other before they came? Did one or two witness something critical on the trip over?

It impressed him that most of them had camped on Cayo Costa before, some many times, and they seemed oddly desperate to return. Perhaps that was why the killer appeared able to be waiting for them, with impeccable timing, striking almost as soon as victims arrived. What drew them? What did they have in common? What drew him?

Libera, Libera, Libera—what to do about you? In Ortillo's gut, since that first poor girl, the violence revolved around Libera. Like most campers, she had reserved a cabin almost a year in advance—plenty of time for a killer to plan, to be waiting.

But, at this early stage, it would be foolhardy to ignore exceptions. Ortillo moved his finger along the Cabin Road, around the loop, to the end of the back row—to a man who had booked his cabin only last week.

Chapter 1

Fred Kenichi should have been the least likely murder suspect imaginable, especially if the murders on Cayo Costa were premeditated. After all, he went to Cayo Costa on the spur of the moment, just to get a couple good nights' sleep. How could he have anticipated that his impulsive trip and solitary presence would make him a murder suspect?

But he was so big—towering and square, with a thick neck, small butt, no gut, and huge hands, that he inevitably attracted attention during the mayhem. And he didn't seem to be camping or fishing or shell collecting like everyone else, not at all. And he was Asian-American.

After Nora died, he stayed in their house in Naples for three years with their black lab, Scout. But when Scout died, Fred couldn't bear the vast emptiness another morning, not another day, so he sold the house quickly, maybe too quickly. He brought only a few essentials to a new condo in Fort Myers—just enough to tide him over until the movers came. Physically, he was in fairly good shape but the days when he would rent a U-Haul and move furniture were long gone.

And there was a problem with the condo. Night after night, he'd lie there on the floor trying to get to sleep. The floor was not the problem; he grew up sleeping on floors. When he bought the place, the complex seemed clean and quiet. But at night, it wasn't quiet, not at all, because a college fraternity was across the street.

For a modest fee, his new super agreed to let the movers in and keep an eye on them for him. Fred didn't want to stick around. Not only wouldn't he feel comfortable watching them work, he wasn't keen about keeping the place. With the noise from the frat house at night, why would he even unpack, when he could just look for a quieter place to live? I'm too old for this nonsense, he thought. And I never felt old before. Not really. I need a break.

Surfing online, he discovered what might be the quietest place in Florida to stay until the movers had left, and it was close by. He'd never been to Cayo Costa, never camped at a state park before, and had no way of knowing how lucky he was to get a cabin, that he had logged on right after a cancellation. He drove to Bokeelia, arrived in plenty of time to catch the boat over, and paid cash without ever making a ferry reservation.

He brought only a sleeping bag and two backpacks. The small one contained minimal clothing, a kit+ bag, matches, a flashlight, two books, and his calligraphy set; the large one held bottled water, three loaves of bread, five apples, a can opener, cutlery, a dish, and five cans of tuna fish. That was it. He couldn't remember the last time that food had tasted good anyway.

He was just going through the motions, doing what had to be done, so that Sunday afternoon, when he entered cabin 9, he was stunned, almost disoriented. The tiny shelter took him by surprise. It was perfect—silent and simple and welcoming.

In her front yard on Grassy Key, just north of Marathon, Libera Grimaldi pivoted and paused, unable to remember what she was supposed to do next. Now, why she was standing there, staring at heaps of camping gear strewn on the lawn? She had been packing for Cayo Costa for days, but, at that moment, she had no idea what she was about to put in the car. What the hell was it? She struggled to remember what she still needed. What was wrong with her? Camping was supposed to be simple. Wasn't the whole idea to leave things behind —no phone, no electricity, no car? What the hell—after all her trips to Cayo Costa, shouldn't she know what she didn't need? How *little* was needed?

Most people would have sworn that she was the least likely murder victim imaginable, especially if a murder was premeditated. At sixty-something, she was a woman of irregular habits, absent-minded and reclusive, independent, and snappish of late. How would any killer know where this scatterbrain might be or what she was liable to do at any given moment? She seldom told anyone what she had in mind and, more and more often, she wasn't sure either. At the very least, she would find it difficult to remember any details.

But she knew her own mind that Sunday morning. She needed, really needed, to get out of the Keys, to get her act together, and the best place to do that was out on Cayo Costa, for at least five days. Five days, because she knew she'd arrive on the island exhausted with all that damned baggage—both material and emotional. She was incapable of traveling light, especially when she camped or kayaked, never could, and the car always looked like a chuck wagon. But this time her psychological funk was worse than ever; it might take a day or so to unwind. But then she'd be free. She cherished Cayo Costa and, even more, she cherished herself there. Miracle of miracles, she even liked other people when she was there, most of them.

As befuddled as she was, and desperately tired, she knew how necessary this trip was, it definitely was—to get to the barrier island's beauty and authenticity, to blessed, safe, at peace and able to focus again. She couldn't wait to watch tarpon swirling in the early morning light, to bike the sandy trails, to marvel at the intricate patterns on sea shells, to play with fire, to listen to mysterious rustlings in the night. Once, when it was pitch black outside, she had seen phosphorescent pinprick-sized lights scattered across the ground everywhere—tiny, tiny lights—maybe insects' eyes—primal and wondrous, like fairy lights.

And time stood still in that wondrous place. Kayaking, fishing, and biking during the day, she would fall into one of the cabin's bunks in the evening and read by headlamp, or write at the simple table. The seclusion was restorative. Even breathing was better on Cayo Costa, sweeter and deeper than it would be anywhere else.

She shrugged. Why not pack everything in sight and organize it later? If she didn't get going, she'd be stuck in the Sunday afternoon traffic on the Overseas Highway and then find herself caught in the Everglades in the dark. She might not arrive in Matlacha until late at night, or maybe she wouldn't even make it that far.

After tossing a package of Oreos onto the dashboard, she tossed a duffle bag, cooler, and backpack into the back. Hopping over a spinning rod, net, and paddle bungeed together on the grass, she shoved a drift anchor, dry bag, and tackle box into a capacious rubber sea bag and hefted it onto the front passenger seat. Seeing space in the back seat, she squeezed a plastic five-gallon bucket holding dish towels and charcoal in and stuffed canned food, meds, books, and a scrub brush on top. She whispered Shakespeare's, "We are such stuff, as dreams are made on," and semi-closed the lumpy bag with carabiners, relishing the freedom to be a slob.

Thankfully, the Tropical Star ferry was good about passengers' baggage. Not only wouldn't she have the energy or the concentration to cull anything at the Bokeelia landing, but she had decided to bring a beach chair on the trip, like most of the other campers. At least she wasn't bringing a pillow. A beach towel stuffed into a pillowcase would do. She'd be embarrassed to be seen with a pillow.

Just then, Mary Alice Fleming, her neighbor, scampered over with a bundle of mail held together with a rubber band. Sport, Mary Alice's yellow Labrador retriever, trotted beside her. "What's up? Going somewhere?" She scanned the mess on the lawn and proffered the packet. "Anyway, before you go—this was in your box, kid."

Libera bristled. "What's this?" and turned away—as though she didn't know.

"If you'd stop pawing all that gear for a moment, this is your cousin's mail." Thinking that Libera might be having one of her lapses, she stated: "This was Nita's last forwarding address, Leeebera." She enunciated and extended the first syllable, hoping to prompt her to think for a moment.

"Put it back." Libera stared at Mary Alice. With that spiked black hair, black shirt, black cargo pants, and compact build, Mary Alice looked like a Pokémon avatar. As lithe and as strong as a gymnast, she could pass for a teenager, although she was pushing fifty. She was a dear friend, delightfully Bohemian, but she did tend to butt in, and sometimes lived up to her brother's nickname for her, "Malice".

"Because Nita passed while she was here, Libera, this is her last forwarding address. So the post office still sends you everything."

"What the hell does 'passed' mean?" Libera shrugged. "Squeaked by with a C minus?"

As tough as Mary Alice could be, she made a face, embarrassed by Libera's insensitivity.

Libera spoke quickly: "Why bother me? She was here for a week, less than a week. Can't her friends up in Machias hang onto her mail? We'll bring her ashes up this summer and toss them off her bluff, or maybe off Mount Desert, say it's a ceremony, and settle things then."

"I take it that you plan to toss the ashes, not her friends in Maine, off the bluff?" Mary Alice asked, trying to lighten the conversation. She could see that Libera was stressed and tired out. "Fill out the form and the post office up there will hold her mail. You *know* that. Get with the program, lady." Mary Alice waggled the packet of mail at her. "You keep forgetting to re-route her mail. You forgot. You forget a lot recently. Should we worry about you-know-what?"

"The day the computer beats me at chess, we can worry. A little memory loss is a blessing—how else could I read great books twice and watch my favorite films again, if I don't quite remember how stories end? You're such a Memory Nazi."

"I just hope you're not losing it." Sport wriggled vigorously. "Not you, Sport-full," Mary Alice cooed. "Libera's lost it. You're spot on." She looked toward the corner of Peachtree and Ferreire. "Well, look who's here, Sportimus."

Sport's best buddy, a Springer Spaniel named Ajax, edged a tall, burly neighbor closer. Without turning around, Libera glimpsed his shock-white hair from the corner of her eye. Bruce "Bounce" Brueghel absently unclipped Ajax's leash, but he didn't pay attention to the prancing dogs. He had been eavesdropping, frowning and intent. A middle-aged, myopic, muscular but pot-bellied man, his unblinking, intense stare occasionally made people uneasy.

When Libera first met him, Bruce mentioned that the kids had nick-named him Bounce in high school, because he bounced the basketball so long before he took foul shots. Even though he tactfully corrected her, she had started calling him "Bounce" all the time. But he didn't care what she called him. She had a mellifluous voice that would entice statues to bend down and listen. He loved her tone, her enunciation, and her expressions. He often listened to her solitary musings and songs while Ajax applied himself. When he drove across the Keys' bridges, he sometimes noticed her kayaking. He daydreamed about this lovely, intriguing woman, and he didn't mind that she seldom talked to him. But he did care, deeply, that perhaps she wasn't well.

Mary Alice glanced down. "Hello there, Ajax old man." Ajax's limp was more pronounced every time she saw him. He just wasn't the dog that he once was, even a year ago. "Our dogs don't live long enough, do they?" she commented.

"Some of them live too long." Libera nodded in the direction of the yapping dogs on the next block. "Noise is exhausting. I'd kill for peace and quiet."

"Go for it." Mary Alice slipped Sport's collar off, and the dogs raced into Libera's yard to explore the odiferous clumps of equipment on the lawn. Ajax resisted the temptation to wrestle with a pile of multi-colored ropes because his teeth hurt, and Sport didn't pee on any gear because that would be wrong. Ajax trotted over to Mary Alice's pickup truck and wistfully checked it out. He had seen Sport jump into the back easily, often— grinning, riding in triumph, sampling scents, showing off. He loved Sport, but he envied his privileges and his youth.

Mary Alice spotted Libera's Keowee kayak on the deck. "Why not take your Eddyline Skylark rather than that beat-up thing?" she asked. "The Skylark's faster, and definitely safer with a spray skirt. As it is, people drop dead wherever you go."

Libera let the last remark pass. "The older kayak is better for fishing— plenty of room for tackle and buckets, and the cockpit is so long and open that I can nap in it. Sometimes I hang that boat between trees like a hammock. It weighs next to nothing." She paused. "Besides, they might scratch the Skylark on the ferry and the Keowee is indestructible. And when I leave it on the rack on Cayo Costa, I don't have to worry that someone might steal it."

"That's for sure. What's with that little shovel?" Mary Alice asked.

"To dig sand fleas, poke the fire pit, swat mosquitoes, toast bread," Libera replied. "By the way, a zillion tree frogs hatched in the water garden overnight. Will you keep an eye on the tadpoles?"

"How, exactly, do you babysit tadpoles?" Mary Alice asked. "Next, you'll ask me to comfort the lizards and beetles that romp around your desk while you're writing—that personal Jurassic Park of yours." She pointed to the left and then into the car: "You have two sleeping bags, know that? One's already in the car. Expecting somebody?"

"Damn," Libera muttered. While Mary Alice poked through her gear, Libera headed to the house with the extra sleeping bag and returned carrying her thirteen-foot yellow kayak with one hand. When she slid the boat onto the car, Bounce studied her. How could his Sun Goddess, with her golden eyes and ash blond hair, be so strong and yet so fragile? As she tossed the ratchet straps across the roof, her child-like, dreamy demeanor mesmerized him.

He did wish that she would button that blouse. Anyone who didn't know her might presume that she was wanton, and that cleavage surely attracted predators. He tried not to imagine what other men thought about her, what they would like to do. And how long would it be before someone took advantage of her absent-mindedness and obvious confusion? If Libera had early-onset Alzheimer's, was this trip a good idea? Several times that month, he witnessed her struggle to follow a line of thought, talking to herself, agitated. He would never forget that last visit to his mother, after her dementia had turned ugly and degrading. She had resembled a fish— mouth open, staring. He never visited her again. He just couldn't.

Mary Alice tightened the bungee around the rod, paddle, and net and propped them up against the car. Libera seemed to break a rod a month. "Why the ferry? Couldn't you paddle over from Jug Creek or Pineland

Road? You're smack dab in the middle of the Great Calusa Blueway up there, you know."

"Can't. Stuff might get wet in the open boat. And what if I'd have to kayak back on Friday and it rains or is rough?" She slid the boat forward on the roof rack and balanced it. "Then what would I do?" She tightened the straps. "As it is, after three days, I have to haul everything from cabin 5 to cabin 12. Those were the only cabins I could get."

"Your blouse? Wrong button," Mary Ann said, leaning into the car, tidying the seat on the passengers' side. "Ever think that buttoning more than one would be a good idea when you travel?"

"When I get there," Libera answered.

"Like I believe that. Your one-button habit is quite an attention-getter for a woman who's seeking peace and quiet." Mary Alice studied multi-colored ropes tangled in a heap on the grass. "Is all this crap from trash? Like most of your stuff? Why not buy yourself new gear, just to see what it's like?"

"I will, after I use up the leftovers. Anyway, I'm going to give up dumpster diving. Not because it's illegal, but because the Sheriff told me that it upsets people."

Mary Alice raised her eyebrows and looked skyward. "When did you start caring about upsetting people?" she muttered as she tied the bow onto the Escort's grill. "I guess it wouldn't do any good to tell you not to speed?"

"It wouldn't," Libera chirped. "You're such a pain in the ass."

Mary Alice started to walk away and half-turned. "Don't forget. Last time, you hit an animal on Route 41 and felt terrible about it. Promise to be careful."

Bounce, walking away in the opposite direction, didn't hear what Mary Alice said, but he clearly heard Libera shout back: "Maybe I killed him, but there was no body when I looked. I'm not sure what happened."

After his shift ended, Detective James Buckman, aka Bucket, drove up to Grassy Key, parked the cruiser in the Mary Alice's driveway and bounded up onto the deck where she sat, repairing a reel. She loved him in uniform. She loved her honey even more out of uniform. With his tufted eyebrows, yellow eyes, tiny pointed nose, trim torso and big shoulders, he resembled a massive owl—placid, smart, and dangerous.

He smirked. After appropriate caresses, he asked, "Libby get off alright?"

"Let's hope, Detective." Mary Alice added, "I caught her taking two sleeping bags."

"Expecting company?" he asked.

"That's the last thing she's looking for—company," she replied. "She's been so antagonistic and surly, acting like everyone pisses her off, that someone might punch her in the nose."

"Hope not. Until last year, we used to worry that she was too naïve and trusting, *too* kind and tolerant. If anything, she seemed oblivious." *

"Except when it came to her cousin Nita."

"Does she realize that people find her hostile?"

"I doubt it." Mary Alice grimaced. "And she wouldn't care. She's not even comfortable with herself."

"That woman needs an angel."

"Several. Let's just hope that she makes it to Matlacha before dark, driving into that sun in weekend traffic. She has trouble with glare, she's impatient, and she's on autopilot when she gets overwhelmed. It's less than a five-hour drive, but she has trouble staying awake from here to Key Largo. And the transmission's acting up."

"Who says? Is she sure about that?"

"Not about the five hours, but she keeps saying that she needs a new transmission. The car bucks."

"Could be spark plugs. Did Andy and Dave's look at it?"

"Not yet. And let's face it—all she had to do was call them and pop down to Marathon. For years, they've nursed that old Escort, knowing how much she needs it to haul boats and salvage trash."

Mary Alice fingered his collar. "Everybody treats her with kid gloves, especially since Nita's death. And, let's face it, no one really knows the whole story. After all, that murder never made sense, especially during the confusion of Fantasy Fest. People baby her, but they talk."

"I could use some babying," he said, moving his chair closer.

"Seriously, Bucky, should she still be driving at night? Is it time for 'The Talk'?"

"Seriously," he answered, "Libera might not take care of eye exams, camping gear, and engines, but she's sharp as a tack when she has to be. Look how she charts and manages solo kayak excursions, disappearing for days. She's just different, in a world of her own—bitchy and irascible, but competent."

"But she didn't used to be such a bitch, not at all. Sometimes she's down-right mean." Mary Alice paused. "And clueless. She'll be lucky to make it home alive."

"Honey, when Nita died, we took a look at Libera's bio and financials. She manages significant assets. Years ago, she socked away a fortune, installing Y2K-compliant systems from Stamford to Siberia. Until recently, she collected royalties for an internal control module."

"Ironic," Mary Alice said. "She's the one that needs internal controls. I'm just saying— clueless."

"Her software monitored employees for decades, fraud *within* companies, even the hours that workers watched porn."

"Good thing that no one who got canned because of that software knows where she lives. She's made enough enemies recently." Mary Alice scuffed at a few Geiger leaves on the deck, and shook her head. "Recently, she's bizarre—somewhere between childhood, fury, and senility."

She smiled and moved closer. "You're not listening, Bucky. Lots could go wrong this week. She's camping on an island without potable water; she kayaks alone on open seas without a spray skirt; and she may be physically able to compete in a senior triathlon, but she's seriously among the missing mentally. She has more hats on the dashboard than a sun-shy hydra." She fingered his badge. "If she weren't so spoiled and selfish, maybe she could cope, but she's a brat. And she attracts attention, the way she bungles the simplest tasks." Mary Alice reached for his top button and purred. "She doesn't know her ass from her elbow."

"I've been having trouble with that distinction myself. Can you help me?"

"Don't be a wise guy. She's heading for trouble. I'd bet on it." Mary Alice lifted her chin high, looked him in the eye, and turned on the heat.

He said, "Let's bet. I'll bet that she stays *out* of trouble, Babe." He brushed his lips against hers and whispered, "Cayo Costa won't have stalkers, trash to steal, or over-consumption to criticize." He sighed, mournfully. "So I'll bet that she'll be OK—if you make the stakes interesting, a win-win situation." He raised his gorgeous eyebrows.

"You're incorrigible."

"Want to discuss the stakes?"

"You bet your ass."

"That's what I had in mind."

Chapter 2

Two days earlier, against all odds, Gilbert Newsome got lucky. Not that way, although that was in the cards. That Friday, in his study in Cape Coral, he logged on to check Monday's reservation for Cayo Cost and found that cabin 8 had become available for Saturday and Sunday also, possibly because rain was forecast. Thrilled that he could score six days instead of four, he nabbed the reservation, tidied his tackle box, checked the reels, and threw a bit of food and many beverages together. He could pick up live shrimp in Matlacha on the way to the ferry the next day. They'd keep, and so would both the wife, "Tough-Tits" Claudia, and the nineteen year-old honey he was juggling.

He packed two sets of clothes: one set for fishing without company and the other for entertaining the honey if she made it over on Tuesday. He almost got caught. Claudia spotted the two camp chairs. "Just habit, dear. But I might as well use the extra chair on the beach for gear, so the sand won't get into the reels and bait. Won't you change your mind and come with me?" He bungeed the chairs together. "You always enjoyed Cayo Costa. I'd bring the new kayak for you. You won't believe how fast that Impex Irie is."

Well-groomed, with streaked blonde hair, small hips, and long limbs, she watched, squinting, her chin thrust forward like a snowy egret zeroing in on a target. That face looks as though it's been through a wind tunnel since she had it done, he thought. He's just a pot-bellied fool with bandy legs, a dyed comb over, and acne scars, she thought.

He grinned. He'd be dead meat if she decided to join him. His idea of a good time didn't ever include Claudia. If all went well, especially if cabin 8 had a screened porch, he and his honey could sit out evenings, drinking and chatting before they got down to business—if she really came. "Bring a book or two," he'd emailed, hoping that she'd catch on, that she'd understand that she should amuse herself while he fished. Right before he slammed out of the house, he emailed: "Take the tram from the landing to cabin 8. I'll be waiting." He didn't want to meet the ferry and embrace Enid in front of people. She might go crazy-affectionate on him. He'd have drinks ready at the cabin. He concluded, "Can't wait, Honey-pie. Cabin 8."

Sipping her morning coffee, dressed in her favorite violet linen chemise, Claudia cruised through Gilbert's email as usual. She had spied on him for years, reading his plans and complaints and phony aspirations, familiar with every one of his personae. It was better than the soaps. But the night before, one remark to this latest chick, about his wife's lack of passion, struck a nerve—after all the workshops and Viagra they'd been through. Claudia told the Yorkie, "He'll pay for this."

Before Gil had pulled out of the driveway, pineshoney@linksnet emailed, "Change of plans! Not taking ferry. Kayaking new Squall from Bokeelia 11:30 Tuesday, meet u at the landing @2:30 can't wait." Claudia erased pineshoney's message immediately, both in *New Mail* and in *Recently Deleted*. She wondered what the new girlfriend looked like.

After Gilbert left, she sat in the kitchen and flipped back and forth from *New Mail* to *Sent*, hoping that he wouldn't check his smart phone and get the chick's message before reaching the island. After that, she could relax. Cayo Costa was a dead zone.

In Bonita Springs, former Chief Financial Officer Philip Schwartz was in a foul mood. First, the grandkids had spoiled his weekend plans, and now he had to take them to Cayo Costa. "Wake them early, so we don't miss the ferry," he ordered Miriam. He removed his glasses, scratched his bald spot, and put his glasses back on.

Like he always does, Miriam thought. If a group of tonsured monks had that habit, they'd resemble chimpanzees. She looked at her hubby— still freckled and big-boned, but sporting a prominent paunch and an attitude. She couldn't wait for him to leave.

She changed the subject. "The boys are in the pool. Swimming might wash some of that grime off the backs of their necks and ankles." She shook her head. "What is she thinking to send them to us like this? I ran their clothes through the washer, except for whatever is in those backpacks. I don't go there."

"This trip is asinine, my dear. The kids don't want to go out to that God-forsaken island, and I really shouldn't go. What if the office calls? What then? I promised to help the team out."

"It's been six weeks since you left, Phil. You haven't heard from them once. They're probably not going to call in the next few days. You're retired. Spend time with your grandsons. Soon, they'll have girlfriends or lacrosse tournaments, and then be off to college before we know it. They won't want to know us then."

"They don't want to know us *now.*"

"I've packed your clothes and put their clean ones in with yours. And the food, water, and campfire supplies are in the car, dear heart. Be sure to bring a good book."

"They don't want to know us *now,*" he repeated. "This is asinine."

After she left the room, he grumbled, "Married forty-six years, and she doesn't know me at all."

"You think?" her voice called back. Then there was no sound but the ticking of the grandfather clock.

"You're going camping this Tuesday? *This* Tuesday? Are you nuts? It'll kill you. You haven't camped out since Girl Scouts." Margot watched Olivia fold the laundry. Extremely tall and thin, with close-cropped red hair and green eyes, her sister was striking, even though she had inherited the longish family nose and small mouth. "What can Cayo Costa possibly offer you that you don't already enjoy here on Sanibel?"

"I'm packed," Olivia said. "I reserved the cabin ages ago. I went there with friends when I was in graduate school and loved it." She grinned. "Actually, you're right. I've really been enjoying life here while he's away." She added. "I keep thinking—this is all so right. I'm so grateful to have this chance."

"You're not thinking." Margot said. She studied her. Olivia looked great. What was up?

Was someone meeting her over there? "Why use vacation days now, to stay a few miles away, when the kids aren't even on semester break? And won't you miss Sean? He'll be back soon."

"Not for one minute. I've discovered that solitude is what I've been waiting for all my life. I take naps. I never have to wait. And you know the best part? I love eating when I want and what I want. I am so grateful."

"But you've always cooked whatever you want. He's good about food. What's the big deal?"

"It's just better alone, better than I ever knew food could taste, is all," Olivia said.

"Mom must be turning over in her grave."

"And that would bother me—why?" She put her hand on Margot's shoulder. "This means a lot to me. I've planned to return to Cayo Costa as long as I can remember. I'm so lucky to have this chance—so many chances." She raised her palms. "The lab's up and running, the patent for the regeneration protein is approved, and I don't have to be anywhere at all." She patted the folded towels. "I've been so fortunate in my life and in biochemistry: so many coincidences led to breakthroughs."

Margot interrupted: "They say that coincidence is a messenger sent by truth."

"Don't you believe in serendipity? I've been lucky, plain and simple, and now I feel grown up, complete. I want to go out and celebrate life."

"OK. I'd say buy me a souvenir, but that's not going to happen out there. So bring me a cockle shell—for a nice soap dish. Does he know you're taking off?"

"He will."

Chapter 3

According to MapQuest, the drive to Matlacha should have taken four hours and forty-five minutes, but it took Libera more than eight hours. It nearly killed her.

Northbound traffic out of the Keys crawled bumper-to-bumper. The Nautical Flea Market on Islamorada accounted for some congestion, and snowbirds and Miami residents left their rentals and second homes at the last moment that afternoon since the weather was simply glorious. Traffic on the mainland was also heavy, even though she took back roads through Florida City and Homestead to avoid the Turnpike. It took her forever to pass a mile-long string of hustling bicyclists hogging the road, all dressed like Spiderman-wannabees, and then she was stuck behind a tractor. Not ten minutes later, she was tied up behind and within a pack of motorcyclists. Most were dressed alike; a few even wore identical beards, badges, and bandanas. Weren't these the very people who considered themselves free spirits, rugged individuals? Would hikers and kayakers adopt uniform dress codes soon? Libera realized that she was being negative, that Mary Alice was right about the bitchiness. She might become a grouch for the rest of her days if she didn't get a life. It worried her.

Now and then, the Escort bucked and stuttered. The Oreos slid from the dashboard to the floor. Why hadn't she brought the car to Andy and

Dave's in Marathon for a check-up? Only I would be this stupid, she thought. When did I stop taking care of business? What if the engine fails in the middle of nowhere? She tried to coast and to leave plenty of space in front, enraging drivers behind her. If she had only packed the day before, and then relaxed all Sunday, slept in her comfortable bed on Grassy Key that night, and left before dawn on Monday, she could have caught the ferry easily—no sweat. Why had she been so anxious to leave?

By the time Libera reached Route 41, the Tamiami Trail, she was hours behind schedule and heading west into a sinking, glaring sun. Furious with herself, she knew that she'd never get beyond the Everglades before dark. To top it off, as soon as she turned onto Route 41, she found herself behind a pickup truck that poked along, a dark shadow leading the way into the blinding sunset. She tried to pass the pickup once, but the Escort bucked and she pulled back. Unable to accelerate sufficiently, driving into the Western glare, she couldn't estimate the distance to pass safely and she couldn't see how fast cars were approaching from the other direction. Other vehicles streamed past the truck and the Escort without apparent difficulty.

The truck driver, presuming that she surely wanted to pass him, wondered what was taking her so long and slowed down, unaware that she was hoping that he'd speed up. There was no choice but to follow him. The exhaust fumes were terrible, noxious and distracting.

And soon a song that her father used to sing to her at bedtime was driving her crazy again. That damned tune had haunted her for weeks; try as she might, she could never remember the lyrics, and now, just when she wanted to think clearly, she couldn't get it out of her head. What if It made her sleepy tonight of all nights? She had to pull herself together.

Then, squinting and trying to concentrate on her driving, she had to contend with an eerie distraction. Incredibly, it seemed that the truck, framed by the setting sun, was carrying two large bobbing bears in the back, their heads haloed in the light, watching her. No matter how hard she tried, she found it difficult to focus on the road, swerving toward the shoulder several times. Was she losing her mind? It was so surreal that it was impossible not to pay attention to those silhouetted bears. Wasn't it in a short story by Tolstoy that two older boys challenged a younger child not to think of a bear, promising him that he could play with them if he could? But, of course, no matter how hard he tried, the little boy couldn't.

"This is ridiculous," she murmured. Were there really bears in the truck? Determined to get a better look and then ignore them, she pulled abreast of the figures for a moment and found to her surprise that the truck really was carrying a three-dimensional diorama of two life-size bears. When headlights approached, she drifted back behind the truck quickly, smiling, thinking that they might as well have constructed a third Baby Bear while they were at it.

By the time the pokey truck with the bears turned off at the Big Cypress Welcome Center, it was pitch dark, she was tired, and her reflexes were shot. I'm beat, she thought. No energy. Nature always wins. Even though reflectors were sunk into the center of the highway, it was difficult to stay in the center of her lane on the black, winding road with no tail lights to follow. She drifted to the right again and again, swerving toward the thin shoulder, unable to drive at the speed limit. When oncoming headlights blinded her, she slowed down to a crawl until they passed. Behind her, faster cars pulled up, tailgating, their headlights blazing into her rear view mirror until they passed, lighting the Escort's interior like extraterrestrial spacecraft.

Concentrating on the road reflectors, ignoring the road looming beyond the headlights and the black sea of grass on either side of her, she felt like crying. Other people do this all the time, easily, she thought. They all stay on the road easily.

Toward the end of the Tamiami Trail, flashing signs ordered her to slow down to 35 mph in Wildlife Endangerment Zones and Panther Crossings. She imagined swerving to avoid an animal and plummeting into the wetlands. Mary Alice once told her that before they erected the fence along the stretch between Key Largo and Florida City, huge snapping turtles used to crawl onto Route 1 at night in the Keys. Hitting one of them, she said, was like hitting a moose. Wouldn't there be turtles and pythons on this road through the Everglades at night? Might she hit one at any minute and plunge off the highway? Would anyone ever find her? A python could swallow and digest her before daybreak. Why did she put herself in these situations?

She was tired and tense, but crying was out of the question. Even though she could see blinking communication towers on the horizon, there was no reception on the radio. She started to whistle oldies; non-stop whistling kept her awake and drove the snatches of Dad's melody out of her head.

If she had only thought to pack the tent, she could have pulled into Collier Seminole Park, just a few miles away. Tent sites were always available there, even choice spots far from the herd of mammoth trailer homes with their gleaming stringed lights. The last time she had camped there, her site was on the very edge of the campground, but RV people spotted her when they went to the showers and word got around. They straggled over to see the lady and her little red tent; some brought leftover steak, beer, and brownies, as though they were feeding wildlife. She smiled, remembering their kindness, and the thought of tucking into a sleeping bag made it even harder to stay awake. She didn't dare stop whistling, even though her mouth was dry. When she approached Naples, she doubted that she had the endurance to reach Matlacha but, after driving around town for twenty minutes, through confusing construction and past No Vacancy signs, she decided to keep going. She stopped for gas, walked around the car three times to limber up, and returned to Rte. 75. I can do this, she thought. I can. And she did.

When she stopped at the Dancing Tarpon Motel in Matlacha, she parked under the floodlights and rested, struggling to get her act together. She knew how spacey she was when she was that tired, especially after dark.

Looking out the window of the motel, Lily May, the manager, wondered why the woman in the car wasn't moving, not coming in. The lady finally opened the car door and hung onto it for a moment, straightened, and shuffled towards the entrance with only a backpack. Lily May hoped that it wasn't another drunk.

Libera thanked her profusely for waiting up. Surprised, Lily May said, "Why, it's not even nine o'clock, Sweetie. But you're most welcome."

When she returned to lock the car, Libera surveyed her cluttered baggage. Was she too old for these trips? At least tomorrow's drive would be a piece of cake—just the short jaunt to Pine Island and the Jug Creek Marina at Bokeelia—less than an hour away, with plenty of time to catch the 1:00 ferry. The instructions said to arrive an hour early. On the ferry, she could forgive herself her trespasses and relax. She couldn't wait. Had peace of mind always been such a function of place for her?

Grateful that the motel door opened with an old fashioned key and not a card, Libera headed to the bathroom and caught a glimpse of herself in the mirror. She looked like Benjamin Franklin on a worn $100 bill. But she had made it within striking distance of Cayo Costa, no small feat, given her muddled and absent-minded frame of mind that afternoon. "Way to be, girl," she told the Benjamin Franklin in the mirror.

The next morning, Libera tucked the motel key in her fanny pack and walked jauntily to a nearby diner. She ordered eggs and toast and relaxed through three cups of coffee, thumbing through a realtors' booklet from a stand at the door. She couldn't remember when breakfast had tasted so good. She edged forward and eavesdropped on a group of five men. They were there when she arrived and looked as though they'd be there if she came back for lunch.

"Soon we'll be taking boats to Cuba."

"My brother went to school with a hippie-type guy who went over to fight with Castro, on that jerk's side in '57, maybe '58, against Battista. Castro gets in, turns Communist, this guy gets tied to a stake in a baseball stadium and shot. And he had fought on Castro's side!"

"If anyone had a little dough, they'd buy all Cuba's old cars. Right away."

On the way back to the motel, Libera approached about twenty fishermen lining the drawbridge—casting, untangling lines, freshening bait, reeling in. Fish were striking.

Libera edged up to a tiny middle-aged woman dressed in Lands' End khaki. She waited until she had cast. "What do you catch?"

"Gimme a minute." She reeled in until the line was taut. "Hi. Inez." She checked her line again. "Snook, redfish, mackerel mostly. Cobia sometimes, seabass when the light's right." She jiggled the rod. "With shrimp. Now and then a sheepshead—best fishing in the country."

"I'm Libera." She peered into the current. "Up north, Rhode Island to Maine, most of the game fish are gone. Giant tuna are so scarce that the Japanese pay $30,000 for a Bluefin. Fifty years ago, during tournaments, they'd hang dozens of them on scaffolds in Galilee and Snug Harbor and then grind them up for cat food and fertilizer."

"That right? It's enough to make you barf the sushi. Big game fish are scarce here, too, but the tarpon are decent." Inez stopped talking. She had a bite, but she didn't strike in time and the line grew slack. Abruptly, the fish stopped hitting.

In the lull, Libera sauntered to the trash barrel near the far end of the bridge. Bundles of tangled fishing lines were discarded among coffee cups, water bottles, and dried shrimp on hooks and leaders. She spotted useable leaders, plastic lures, and a dandy silver spoon, and took a pair of scissors from her fanny pack to cut the loot loose.

"What the hell do you think *you're* doing?" a fisherman next to the barrel asked. Heads swiveled to watch the woman with a one-button habit riffling through the trash. Hurrying, Libera bundled the line and the gear together, along with some unavoidable garbage and dead bait; she dangled the salvage from her hand, lost for words.

"Wait a minute, Lady. My boy here does the barrels. That gear adds up. Go price the stuff. It's ours, even that piece of bagel for the dog."

Caught shrimp-handed, Libera fled, walking quickly and then breaking into a trot as she ran a gauntlet of irate and curious anglers. She chided herself: what if everyone behaved this way? But I just can't help it, looting feels so right. "She's at the motel," she heard a man shout.

Back at the Dancing Tarpon, Libera poked through the loot, discarded 95% of it, and stuffed the keepers into an empty Ziploc bag from her backpack. She peered out of the Venetian blinds. No one was in sight. Exhilarated, she headed to the office and checked out. The weather on the drive to Pine Island couldn't have been nicer.

At the Jug Creek Chandlery, the clerk informed her: "No ma'am, your ferry *to* Cayo Costa is for 2:00, not 1:00. You have it backwards. The ferry *from* Cayo Costa leaves at 1:00. You can leave your bags, cooler, and kayak on the dock now, though."

"No problem," Libera said. "I might dash back to the Pine Island library, get some magazines, and catch up on email. May I pay for parking now? Here's my credit card."

"Pay now, and then leave your car in ferry parking when you get back from the library. Give us the key then, Sweetie, in case we have to move it."

Libera was delighted to be carefree and early for a change. Driving back up H. Stringfellow Street, she couldn't remember when strangers started calling her "Sweetie". Maybe it was when Hispanics began to call her "Mommy". She wondered who H. Stringfellow was. Had she ever seen a street sign with a person's first initial before? It didn't faze her when she reached the library and discovered that it was closed on Mondays. She used a portable *Pour Toi* at the ball field nearby and drove back to wait for the ferry, singing *Everybody Loves Somebody Sometime,* on time, no rush.

At Jug Creek, she lugged her bags and gear to the wharf, slid the kayak off the roof rack, and stowed the life jacket behind the seat. A dry bag with a change of clothing, two apples, and a small Plano tackle box was already stuffed into the bow; the old boat had no dry wells. Gradually, a size-able crowd gathered at the dock, and by the looks of their baggage, many might be staying the two-week limit. Backpacks, coolers, beach chairs, fishing gear, sleeping bags, and pillows were piled into stacks near the pier. Somehow, Mary Alice, without asking, had tied pieces of yellow shoe laces on Libera's luggage, every piece, even on the bungeed rod, net, and paddle, so that nothing could go wrong.

Chapter 4

Libera dragged the kayak to the edge of the wharf, politely refusing help from two men who stood by a pile with four fishing rods, three coolers, two camp chairs, and two raggedy backpacks that looked half empty. They introduced themselves—Mason and Will. Mason had an Appalachian accent. Since they didn't pack a tent, she presumed that they had a cabin.

Will smiled. "Bartender, real estate, boat yard, sixty, fun and trouble in cabin 6," he told her, a questioning look in his blue-green eyes.

"Kayak, snappers, poetry, peace and quiet in cabin 5," she shot back, grinning, flirting, dazzled. He was so damned handsome and weathered, so tall and solid. *Razzle dazzle 'em,* she thought, thinking of lyrics from the musical Chicago, mesmerized. He's got it down pat and I love it. He's adorable. She realized that she couldn't stop smiling; she hadn't felt a buzz like that in so long. She felt alive, yet at rest.

In the midst of this epiphany, Libera played with the zipper on her fanny pack and realized that she had startled herself. Why not reach out more often? How many times had she regretted her lack of courage, not speaking up, skipping those twenty-second answers that often made all the difference? How often she had regretted being on guard and abrupt for no reason at all—why not reveal herself, why not share the obvious? "I'm shy, please give me a moment," or "I'm not sure what I want" or "I'll have to think about that"?

She stared at Mason. Why *not* take her chances like everyone else? Listening more, concocting an occasional friendly overture wouldn't kill her. What did she have to lose? It had been a while since she even noticed how sweet and interesting people were. Why the inattentiveness, why the attitude, anyway? She'd had a joyous life, joyous and privileged, but craven in the past few years. That chip on her shoulder was craven. Try me, she thought. Come on brothers and sisters, children and beasts, try me. She realized that she was smiling.

A couple with two grown sons, one wearing a Wiscasset T-shirt approached. "Hey, we're from Bangor," the father said.

"Machias," she replied, "Just summers." But maybe she wouldn't wear the hat with the Maine logo again, unless she was in Maine. Then she stared at Will. He rocked her—rough-hewn but clean-shaven, buzz-cut hair, very large in the shoulders and arms. His rumpled khakis seemed just right. She moved closer and listened to him, drinking in his deep bass tones. He didn't seem to mind.

"Katherine's madder than hell," Will told Mason.

Mason apparently didn't want to go there. "'Bout time you and I went camping anyway, without the boys, by ourselves." He stroked his stubble.

"So she says, 'Three days. If you stay one day more, don't come home.' That woman don't want me around, and she don't want me home either."

"Now Buddy, we both know, there's been a lot of water pass under that bridge. Third time around, old buddy. And she's not so bad." Mason seemed to be chewing something. "Water under the bridge. Let's just have us a really good time and forget home for a while."

"Four days. Four whole bitchin'' days," Will added. "We are *so* friggin' free." He peered into the largest cooler. "Watch the stuff. I'm going into the fish house and buy us a nice redfish for dinner tonight, before we go surf casting."

Libera studied the crowd, waiting for the ferry, not minding the wait. Parents juggled infants, adjusting their little hats. Three leashed and muzzled dogs panted in the noonday heat. When she heard Russian, she turned to study a family of two men, two small boys, and a stunning coiffured woman wearing lipstick and mascara. It had been quite a while since she had people-watched, a long time. How thoughtful, how poignant, these people seemed—everyone there just wanted a good life for themselves and their loved ones. How quietly everyone chatted. How fragile we all are, she thought. I should get out more often.

Passengers clustered under the meager shade of the fish house. A boy in a faded red T-shirt gently piled a folded stroller, a guitar, and a baseball bat next to her Keowee. Two women with billowing Hawaiian print skirts approached with three toddlers in tow. "May the children touch the boat?" the taller one asked. "I'm Harmony. This is my sister Hope."

"Of course," Libera answered. "Sit right on the bow, kids, unless the sun's too much." The boy in the red T-shirt discreetly moved the guitar away from the two oldest toddlers who began plopping up and down on the kayak. They drank from identical sippy cups while the baby watched solemnly and then the little group drifted away. Day trippers, Libera thought—diaper bags and beach chairs—no luggage. Where did young mothers get the energy to travel with babies?

A group gathered around four very thin girls in very minimal shorts. Mason must have sensed that Libera was close behind him, because he turned and told her: "Those kids from U. Va. just got a $300 speeding ticket in Matlacha. What a way to start their spring break." Libera noticed that the coeds had four coolers—four coolers for just four girls.

When the ferry arrived, it resembled a flat-roofed green bus. The call of the osprey on a nearby pole, the crabs scooting around the pilings, the wake of a passing boat, the sight of the mate wrapping, tugging, and rewrapping the lines to secure the ferry—everything occurred with such clarity and unhurried deliberation, it was lovely. After a handful of passengers disembarked—a bit disheveled and seemingly content, the crew slid the Keowee onto the ferry's roof and began passing everyone's luggage forward, except for the bicycles which they rolled aft. She was the first passenger on board and sat next to the mate, near the exit, so that she'd be the first to get off and collect her boat. She knew the routine. She was comfy, nestled among duffle bags and chaises, jugs and back packs, the guitar, a tea kettle, and sixteen coolers. More were probably stowed under the benches.

After the ferry cast off for the 55-minute voyage, the mate collected fares. He took his time, first checking off those who had reservations and passing out green slips for the return voyage. Day trippers tended to pay cash, and campers tended to use credit cards, probably the same ones that they had used to make their reservations.

Two young boys, alternately poking and whispering to each other, sat next to a dapper man dressed like Arnold Palmer. Libera sensed that they might be making derogatory remarks about their grandfather. He looked grim.

Two black women who appeared to be in their late twenties sat leaning on each other, holding hands: "Melony and Keisha," they told the mate. With their close-cropped Annie Lennox hair, tank tops, and cargo pants, Libera thought that she'd have trouble telling one from the other if she met them separately. Keisha spoke to Melony quietly, discussing her parents. "This area was their stomping ground, if you could call what they did 'stomping'." She pursed her lips. "In their sixties, from Christmas to Easter, year after year, until they couldn't afford it anymore, Mom and Dad stayed on either Sanibel or Captiva, living for that morning coffee in the room, shell collecting, day trips, and dressing for dinner. But they never considered camping, especially not in a state park. So, eventually, they couldn't afford to come any more."

A buxom woman with an ear-budded daughter and an inquisitive Schnauzer offered a hand to Melony. "Lily, from Ontario, just left Grayson Beach. We tent at two Florida parks a year."

"Ontario, Canada? Try Myakka sometime, near Sarasota. It's the best," Melony suggested. "We're camping on the Dry Tortugas next month, but that's a bit far for you and it's really, really bare bones, all tents, no cabin, probably no dogs."

Eavesdropping, Libera presumed that the Canadians had driven all the way down, since they had the dog. There was something about Canadians that she really liked—never full of themselves, you could tell.

It was quiet on ferry. Even in Matlacha, when those men told her not to stop going through the trash, and in Bokeelia when she was waiting for ferry, it had seemed quiet, a prelude to the imminent peace she craved.

On board, couples and groups chatted about manatees and stingrays, blue herons and tarpon and mullet, seashells and the Pioneer Cemetery. After a day or two, after they had fished side by side during the day and sat together around fire rings at night, they'd discuss matters closest to the heart: wayward children, amicable divorces, aging parents, office politics. What is it about staying on Cayo Costa that provides perspective? They'd ask. Finally, they'd say how much they hated to leave. They felt alive and free, so innocent there. That's why most of them came back again and again. That's why she had come.

She was grateful that no one played music. She loved a quiet passage, the looks that passed between partners, the snatches of conversation. She was surprised to overhear Will discuss Marjorie Rawlings' *The Yearling* with the coeds: "So her agent told her to piece a book together from her letters to him, and it's still a classic. You have to write about what you know."

"Yeah, but we don't know anything. We hand in stuff that we find on the internet," the tallest coed, the willowy girl named Sue, answered.

A somber child balanced between a row of benches, not looking for a seat, his mouth down-turned. Libera thought that he was affecting his slight limp. He was a veritable *Where's Waldo* look-alike, with freckles, thick glasses, ears like satellite dishes, and wild flaming hair. He clutched his towel and scowled at his parents ahead of him, if that's who they were. He clearly wanted everyone to know that the couple did not meet with his approval. Fifteen minutes into the trip, Waldo won Libera's sympathy when the presumed mother toyed with the hair on his presumed father's arm, the man rested his hand on her thigh, and the woman then slithered onto his lap and nuzzled him. Libera grinned at Will when he caught her eye.

The Virginia quartet sat at the end of the opposite row, near the bicycles. The girls shared a tiny bag of trail mix and two huge bags of potato chips. Libera strained to hear snatches of their conversation. It helped that they talked with their hands.

"I'm not missing Facebook yet, not at all," a freckled redhead named Mary said. "Are you guys still keeping your word? A whole week without social media? How about you, Sue?"

Applying lip gloss, a twig-thin coed paused, ran her tongue over her lips, paused again, and asked, "Does it count if I still Twitter in my head, even though I'm not texting? I always think Twitter. In my head, I twit. It's how I think."

"That's so lame." The tiniest coed, doe-eyed Tiana shrugged, extended her legs, and studied them. Shaking her head, she confided to a lugubrious girl on the end of the bench, "Asian and Russian girls luck out. Men love girls whose thighs don't touch, Rosie."

"Who gives a shit," Rosie drawled, reaching for Sue's lip gloss. "The Asians have small tits."

Libera noticed little Waldo studying the girls. And they began to study him. Suddenly, Tiana called to him, "Hey, do you know that you look like Waldo. We love Waldo!"

Waldo pretended that he didn't hear, but it was obvious that he was pleased. After a minute or two, he announced: "You can call me Waldo."

On a set of tiered benches facing the front of the ferry, what appeared to be a wolfhound-poodle mix sat next to a grinning boy, Roger Templeton. The huge dog purposely edged the child to the end of the bench, little by little, just pausing once to lean over and lick the cheek of Roger's mother Sharon, who was eating a banana on the dog's other side. "Wolf!" she protested, pulling her snack away from his massive tongue. Wolf then turned and shoved Roger down the bench again, but when Roger teetered on the edge of his seat, halfway off, the boy pushed back, sliding the hound in the other direction. Then he affably tilted the dog's head up so that the makeshift bandana muzzle wouldn't slip off. Having fun, he swung his greenglow sneakers back and forth; there were identical matching stipes on the sleeve of shirt. His beautiful, chubby sister, Mia, sat on Mrs. Templeton's other side and grinned at the dog's antics, coyly showing the audience that the handsome beast was hers too.

The captain and the mate discussed the fee for delivering the three boxes of groceries stacked on a bench close to the wheel. "Nautilus" was written on each box. Probably meant for long-term campers or volunteers, Libera thought. Or maybe "Nautilus" was the name of a residence, a cottage, a boat, or a metaphor—like Oliver Wendell Holmes' chambered Nautilus.

Libera was the first passenger off the boat. The mate held out his hand to help her step down, and she hustled down the pier to fetch one of the wheelbarrows for her gear. Within five minutes, she had dragged the Keowee to the private kayak rack and loaded her stuff into the bed of a truck with two linked trams attached. She climbed into the first row, holding her rod-cum-paddle upright after the uniformed driver said, "Bikes in the truck, cabins in the front tram, tents in the second, please." Libera heard him tell Melony and Keisha that his name was Richard, a volunteer, and that most of the park was staffed by volunteers; there were only four rangers. He sometimes worked at Bahia Honda State Park, too. What a nice way to live, she thought. She sat and felt tension flow out of her and out of her, like the change of the tide.

The mate loaded four jugs of water and the Nautilus's groceries onto the truck with other baggage. He told Richard, "These groceries go to the intersection."

"Did everyone register in the Rangers' Office?" A petite staffer walked up to her, so close that Libera could read her name tag—Molly Standish.

"I didn't." Libera slowly descended and headed toward the hut where she had checked in on her last visit.

"Not there," Richard called. "There." He pointed.

"Why you have the new building now, you finished it," Libera said.

"New digs," Molly replied. She turned to the other passengers, "While the lady registers, you can purchase wood and ice at the store right there, beyond the restrooms."

The Rangers' Office was nearly bare, with just a counter, a rack of brochures, and a diorama showing a nesting turtle and hatching eggs. The petrified hatchlings looked real and grisly. Libera wondered if they had used a broken nest for the display.

She read Ranger Jonathan Edwards' name tag and began, "I'd like. . . ,"
when she was interrupted by a large middle-aged man who rushed in, jutting the chin of his massive bald head in front of her.

"Oscar Coleman. We'd like to stay in cabin 7 until Sunday."

"Let's see." The Ranger shuffled through his clipboard and then studied the whiteboard behind the desk. The Colemans had reserved cabin 7
for only two more nights, until Wednesday. "Sorry. It looks like someone
has reserved 7 for Wednesday through Sunday."

"But we'd kill to stay longer. Our ancestors lived here." Oscar placed
his palms flat on the counter. "Is there any chance that they might cancel?"

"Probably not. We won't know until 1:00, Wednesday. Check then.
Maybe there'll be another cabin," said Ranger Edwards. "But I doubt it."

"I'm keeping the tram waiting," said Libera. She studied a whiteboard
listing the rangers, their photos, and their assignments. Killing time, she wondered where Rangers Jonathan Edwards, Tomás Hernandez. Esme White and
Frederick Bartholomew slept, and whether their families lived on the island also.

Oscar ignored her. "We'd prefer not to move to a different cabin. Can't
you put the new people in another cabin?"

Ranger Edwards answered: "It doesn't work that way," and turned to
Libera.

"I'd like to register, please. Libera Grimaldi. Three nights in cabin 5,
and one night in cabin 12—Monday and Tuesday and Wednesday, and
then Thursday, departing Friday."

"No problem," he said. She wondered if people mentioned the eighteenth
century Jonathan Edwards to him and drove him crazy. He shuffled through
papers on a clipboard. "Well. Let's see." He paused and pointed at the papers.
"OK. But we have you for only one night in 5, and three nights in 12."

"That's fine, even better," she said, wondering if his parents were puri-
tanical, the poor guy, and absently tucking the trail and cabin maps into
her shorts. "Even better," she repeated. "When do I move to cabin 12?"

"We'll help. Tomorrow, after the couple in 12 checks out. Around noon OK?"

"Great," Libera said, pleased that she'd settle in early and be free to kayak all Tuesday afternoon. She returned to the tram and sat in front next to the golfing grandfather. She couldn't hear what the five Russians were saying in the back rows, but it sounded conspiratorial and her imagination started working overtime. There was room for one more person in front, but the truck started with a whine and a roar and headed down the Cabin Trail.

The golfer introduced himself as Phil Schwartz, in cabin 1. He seemed like a lovely man. With their feet up on the back of his seat, his grandsons were crammed into the bench behind them, next to a portly gentleman with two bags of ice who shouted to the driver, "Gilbert Newsome, cabin 8," and turned to the older boy, "I came Saturday."

The boy volunteered, "I'm Morgan. The pathetic tosser next to me is Sebastian. Sebby." As the tram rumbled along, Morgan told Gilbert, loud enough for Libera and Phil to hear, "Pops is a Gated Community Organizer." Sebby snickered. "You should see his place. 6,000 acres laid out like a Monopoly board and nothing to do except walk up and down the streets every morning. It's like The Stepford Seniors—only three types of houses, every yard alike, caged pools like aviaries," Morgan added. "It's simply enigmatic." He loved that word.

"We call it 'Poppy's Zoo'," the tosser piped up.

A woman with an older man, sitting behind the boys, bent forward: "We're in cabin 2, Mary Ellison and Spencer Clark, retired professors," she said. Spencer leaned back. There goes Mary again, elbowing me, always the do-gooder—trying to curtail that idiot grandson's hurtful remarks. Spence studied Mary, Mary studied the boys, and Morgan studied her. Mary noticed a scar on his left eyebrow, old scabs on his knees and elbows, and a black brace on his right wrist. Skateboarding? His shorts were baggy and worn as low as decency permitted. Definitely skateboards, she thought. He grinned. Sebby didn't turn to look at her.

Suddenly there was a commotion in the woods on their right. "A wild pig," exclaimed a girl behind the professors. The tram stopped and Libera heard crashing in the woods.

"Good eye, Melony." Keisha nudged her lightly.

They drove through pin oaks, pines, oak-palms, and finally, to sandy scrub. Melony noticed that Mary Ellison eyed the boys more than the scenery.

Campers in the rear wagon clambered off at the intersection leading to the tent sites. First, the Templeton trio from Canada stepped down, with every-thing they needed strapped to two massive mountain backpacks, followed by their celebrity wolfhound; and then Waldo's family, except for Waldo. He didn't move until after the coeds jumped off and began dragging their coolers, one on top of the other; then he followed them down the sandy trail to the tents.

As if on cue, the girls chanted:

Rosie, Mary, Tiana, and Sue
Just be nice to us,
And we'll be nice to you.

Delighted, tucking his head down, without missing a beat, Waldo whispered:

Rosie, Mary, Tiana, and Sue,
Stick with Waldo, and he'll
Teach that Matlacha policeman a thing or two.

The girls whopped, turned, and waited for him to catch up and walk with them. He picked up their smallest cooler and carried it on one shoul-der. They squealed with delight. No one else had heard him.

A jovial couple with four barefoot children, an old beagle, and a dolly waded forward to collect the groceries. The Nautilus family, Libera surmised. She was surprised that the mother wore a housedress. Day trippers descended from the second tram and carried their chairs, coolers, towels, and umbrellas toward the beach path. Libera wondered if they would collect all the best shells before she got there. Harmony and Hope walked away slowly, letting the toddlers pick up stones and finger the sand at the edge of the road. A heavy woman laboriously disembarked with a cane, and shouted after a stout man heading up the path that she couldn't keep up, she still had blisters. Head down, he waited, but didn't look back at her.

In the lull, Libera overheard Melony and Keisha tell the professors that they were in cabin 4 and had stayed on Cayo Costa several times before. She wondered when they worked.

The tram drove the few hundred feet to the cabins, and the golfing grandfather and his two restive grandsons climbed off at cabin 1. The boys grabbed small backpacks, firewood, and the ice. Libera wondered if they had packed any other clothing.

"Would you please carry our wood and ice, too?" Mary asked them. "We're next to you, in 2." Morgan nodded, smiling, and carried the couples' wood and ice to their porch while Mary and Spencer unloaded two backpacks, two coolers, and four briefcases: "You can take the professors out of the university, but you can't take the university out of the professor," Mary joked. "Thank you."

Libera thought that Spencer probably had a back hip or a bad knee. For some reason, perhaps the tilt of his head or his inquiring gaze, she thought that he might also have bad hearing. On the other hand, Mary bounced around like an advertisement for Celebrex.

Phil walked up to his cabin and turned, "You boys go play now."

"Can't we see the inside of the cabin first, Pops?" Sebby asked.

"Well, carry the stuff in then. Choose a bunk. Then go play."

The tram drove past cabin 3, which seemed empty, the key in the door. Melony and Keisha were dropped off at cabin 4, Sea Breeze. Their minimal luggage looked like it had been packed professionally.

In the murder investigations during the next four days, Detective Ortillo's team interrogated every adult cabin and tent camper but one. Most recollections and impressions were robust and precise, but he was convinced that Mary Ellison was holding something back.

Chapter 5

Without being asked, the Russian men bowing and introducing themselves as Boris and Paul Rodzianko, unloaded Libera's baggage at cabin 5. "Sasha and Stas," Boris told her, nodding toward the boys who were whooping and scampering across the loop to the road in back, to see what cabin 11 was like.

Cabin 5 had no screened porch, so Libera heaved her paddle, rods, and net directly up onto the floor as the tram chugged away. The previous campers had tied a rope high across the posts, probably as a clothesline, and the porch floor was scorched in the front corner in the shape of a mosquito ring. The area had been raked, but a bottle cap and chunks of scorched firewood were left in the fire ring. Libera spotted a twist tie under the edge of the porch, and there were fragments of sea shells under the picnic table. I'm picky, she thought, but I want everything to be perfect, at least here.

Inside, the cabin was perfect. It really was. The little shack was swept and immaculate, and smelled like fresh-cut lumber. Six bunks, six mattresses, a picnic table, and small built-in shelves in each front corner—all for her. The amenities felt excessive in that primitive place, too much for just one person, but she was delighted. All that she needed in life was right here. Propped-up shutters shaded the interior, protection against both rain and the heat of the day—like hotels in Paris and Florence, she recalled. The shutters were probably never closed and hooked shut unless there was a hurricane, she mused. The cabin was named Sea Fan, very *feng sui*. Perfect.

Libera piled a second mattress onto the bottom bunk in the far corner. The beefed-up bed looked inviting, but she wanted to check out the beach before dark so she decided to hike to the south end for a trifecta: fishing, shell collecting, and watching the sunset. I'm back, she thought. I'm here.

Behind her, the occupants of cabin 10 were noisy. It sounded like they had many small children. Perhaps they'd quiet down by the time she returned from the beach. Eager to get to the shore, she plopped defrosted squid and shrimp into a Ziploc, put an empty pill bottle containing hooks and weights in the five gallon bucket, and untied the spinning rod from the paddle. She left a flashlight on the front step, piled charcoal in the grill, and placed a butane light wand and a pop-up can of ravioli on the grill's shelf. It was amazing how that delicious canned food always tasted when she camped; she wouldn't dream of eating from a can at home.

"Fishing?" Will called from the porch of cabin 6. "We're surf casting later. Join us."

She waved and headed up the road. At cabin 1, Sea Oats, Phil Schwartz watched Libera approach—such a pretty, purposeful woman. She looked joyous, as though she'd start skipping at any moment, and she had to be in her sixties. That gal probably was carefree every day of her life. He kicked off his spiffy Tommy Bahama loafers, sat back in his beach chair on the screened porch, and began to read Captain J. Kirk Walker's *Boat Goat,* about Pine Island Sound's history. At the store, he had seen Professor Clark also buy a copy but he didn't have a chance to talk to him because Morgan tugged his sleeve.

"Can we have $10 to go kayaking sometime, Pops?"

"What?" Phil asked, startled.

"May we please have $20 to rent two kayaks, Pops?"

"Here's $40, boys. Rent bikes, too."

"When?" asked Sebby.

"Anytime, boys. Today, tomorrow, anytime."

Walking away, Sebby said to Morgan: "He doesn't want us around. And he never says my name. Does he know my name? It's just 'boys' this, and 'boys' that."

"So we do whatever we want, as long as we don't drown or something. That works. We're free. And if you can't keep up with me, I'm not waiting."

Pleased that there were interesting adults around, Phil watched Libera turn onto the path to the beach while the girls from cabin 4 rolled bikes onto the dirt road. The kids weren't going to be a bother. Morgan could light the grill himself and roast the hot dogs later. He remembered how much fun it was to build a roaring fire when he was a boy. Feeling their oats at Sea Oats, he thought. He was stunned that they weren't pestering him. Perhaps he wouldn't have to pay attention to them at all. In fact, when he looked around, he had no idea where they were or when they were coming back.

Libera passed the pavilion used for lectures and sing-alongs and glanced at a bulletin board with exhibits and posters across the road. One illustrated the island's fauna: the gopher tortoise, marsh rabbit, brown pelican, coach whip snake, armadillo, black racer, and wild pig. She'd love to see an armadillo. Another poster featured shorebirds; she studied the pictures and descriptions of the killdeer and sanderling, but she knew that she'd struggle to remember their names when she saw them; she was bad with birds. A glass case contained a sea shell exhibit; she knew most of them. She scanned two notices: a guest speaker, a botanist, had presented a slide show that afternoon, and there was a star walk that night. She'd go if she was still awake, unless the full moon had already risen.

On the beach, heading south, she noticed fresh trenches in the soft sand, up toward the dunes, not at the water's edge. Why would someone dig so far up above the high tide mark, when sand fleas burrowed down at the water line? She realized that she had forgotten her shovel and flashlight back on the porch, as well as the squid and shrimp on the steps. So she was lugging the rod around for nothing—no sand fleas, no bait, and it would be dark soon.

Behind her, toward the north end of the beach, a photographer was posing a couple at the edge of a dune. Even at that distance, it was clear that the woman wore a wedding gown. A group stood to one side, apparently waiting; probably the family, Libera thought. Could the couple have been married on the island? The sunset would provide a beautiful backdrop for the picture.

Directly ahead, at the point, the beach was seriously eroded; at the edge of the new bluff, piles and piles of giant cockle shells, crown conch, and whelk shells were exposed. What luck! Perhaps the storm three days earlier was responsible for the bonanza. She often used large shells for baked stuffed clams but no longer set them out for ash trays. Here and there, stunning lightning and pear whelks were undamaged. Thrilled, she clawed at the exposed bluff, hoping to find a translucent jingle shell or a rose petal tellin. The bucket came in handy but there were so many olive shells, Florida clams, zigzag scallops, and angel wings that she soon ignored them and became more selective. Gathering treasures, she forgot about the time until it became difficult to see in the fading light. Yet, as soon as she resolved to hustle back, she spotted a spiny jewel box shell and then an alphabet cone to add to her collection.

If she plowed through the thick sand above the water line, it would take ages and she'd be out there in the dark. The packed sand at the water's edge was littered with spiny urchin shells and she was barefoot, but that was the fast way back And why had she lugged all that fishing gear, why wasted time at the exhibits and posters? At least, she should have brought the flashlight and sandals.

At the edge of the gray surf, the damp sand reflected the magnificent sunset. The sky morphed from a golden rose to an orange-scarlet to vermilion with patches of blue-green. Here and there at the foaming surf's edge, terns scrambled, feeding assiduously. The sun shrank and slipped beneath the horizon. How small the earth, she thought; how quickly and quietly the sun sets at the very end, like our days. Ahead of her, two couples watched the moment. Beyond them, a large group clustered in rows of beach chairs, arranged as though for a concert. Tenters, she surmised. If I was a normal and giving person, I suppose that I'd want to share this glory with someone, too. But I'm not and I don't.

In the dusk, it was more and more difficult to see clearly and when she tried to skirt the urchin shells, she hopped right onto one. The spines stuck into the pad of her foot rather than the delicate ball, but it really hurt. Only the first day, and she had messed up.

Limping on her way back to the cabin, she decided to get her act together: clean up, eat quickly, get some sleep, and unpack the next day after moving into cabin 12. She could fish at first light, pile her things on the cabin 5's porch, take the tram to the landing after moving, and kayak all afternoon—first to Pelican Bay and then to the lagoon with the manatees. There was so much to look forward to. For most of the day, she'd rest her foot and enjoy the solitude.

At the restroom facilities behind cabin 5, next to cabin 12, the women's bathroom was on the right, not on the left like the facilities at the landing. She reminded herself to be careful not to go into the Gents. She rinsed both feet under the spigot, and peered at the Russians at cabin 11. All five of them were gathering armfuls of stiff coco plum leaves, probably for kindling. It was impossible to tell which man the woman was with; one of them called her Tamara. She looked like a model, her head expertly wrapped in a scarf; one of the men looked equally exotic, with flamboyant Aladdin-type balloon pants.

"Boris," she heard the woman call. "It's late."

Libera tried to hold the flashlight first in her teeth and then under her chin, to get a closer look at her foot.

"May I help?" A large man gently reached for her elbow as she tried to keep her balance on her good foot. Fred Kenichi had noticed Libera when she left the Rangers' Office and again from cabin 9's porch when she walked to the beach before sunset. How lovely she was. So lovely, so bewitching, that he overcame his shyness.

"Do sea urchins leave spines?" she asked.

"Maybe," he replied. "Let me hold the light for you. Lean on me."

She rested against him. He was stunning. Where had he come from? It seemed as though he radiated power, peace, and gentleness—like an aura. It took her breathe away. At my age, she thought. She wanted to linger, to learn more about him, but she couldn't examine the wound while she was standing up.

"I'll take a closer look back at my cabin. Thanks." She paused. "Libera," she told him.

"Fred," he answered. He wished that he could kiss her hand. At my age, he thought.

To avoid getting dirt in the wound, she limped along the road to her cabin rather than cut through the brush. She waved to a couple sitting by the fire ring at cabin 12.

"Can you use ice?" A large woman wearing a soiled apron over shorts called. "We're leaving tomorrow."

"I'm moving into your cabin tomorrow, actually," Libera told them.

"Sit with us," she urged. "Let's get a look at you. I'm Dolores, and my better half is Ralphy. Use the picnic table bench." The three admired the fire in silence until Dolores said, "We love it here." She spoke sweetly. "This afternoon I read Timothy. As in Ecclesiasticus, time and water flow as a system, down to the sea." Libera wondered if the disciple Timothy had really used the word "system", but she enjoyed the imagery and Dolores' lack of guile. She learned that Ralphy was a retired auto worker and that the couple moved around the country in a trailer home, working odd jobs when necessary.

"Can you use bottled water too? We'll leave some. Too bad we didn't save a bit of mullet. Cooked over the fire with roasted corn, it was incredible," Ralphy said. He put his arm around his wife.

Libera smiled. Where else could I meet such lovely people? Mary Alice might make fun of these scruffy religious nomads. Tranquil, she watched the fire for a while, and then bid the couple a good night and a safe journey, thanked them for the ice and water, and left.

Her wound was gritty with sand by the time she returned to cabin 5 and lit the fire. Sitting on the porch steps, she iced the wound and then probed for urchin spines. The can of beef ravioli heated in minutes, even before the charcoal's flames subsided. Famished, she ate slices of Publix's mountain bread from the bag while the pasta cooled. Then she ate Chef Boy 'R Dee with more bread and the last of her butter, using a Frisbee for a plate and a spoon from the sleeve of the cooler. She had forgotten to pack dishes and flatware.

She limped back to the restroom and filled the bucket at the outside tap. Her foot was killing her. She held it under the spigot again, and wondered— was I always this careless? Then she stood for a moment, serene. She had made it to Cayo Costa, already collected a treasury of shells, met generous and lively travelers, and eaten forbidden food like a wild child. And she was free, totally free. She decided to build a roaring fire the next night, a fire like Dolores' and Ralphy's, a fire so big that she could heat breakfast coffee over the embers the next morning. But she never got the chance.

The moon had not yet risen. On the bunk next to hers, Libera placed a backpack and sweatshirt within easy reach. The room smelled wonderful, like fresh lumber. She slipped into her bunk, holding her book to her chest, careful not to hit her head. Above her, someone had written: "When someone tells you who they are, believe them." She studied it. Was it a cautionary note? A suitor declaring himself? Just a favorite Maya Angelou quote? It looked like a woman's printing, but she couldn't be sure. She placed her glasses at the head of the abutting bunk, turned off the light, and slid it under her pillow.

At rest, savoring the dark, sensuous, she felt unbound in a special insularity, not quite immortal, but as though she had all the time in the world to rest and think and explore. She monitored her body: the heartbeat, the symmetry, the latent power, the grace. Her eyes were not becoming accustomed to the dark. Was the night that black? Either there's a heavy cloud cover or the moon is rising late, she thought, because there was a full moon that week, the reason she had come on those dates. She couldn't remember the last time she had stood and watched the moon.

She had been interested in the dark since grammar school, when she read a biography of Louis Braille and his tactile language for the blind, invented in 1855. As a girl, she practiced being blind in case she lost her sight too, someday. This became a life-long habit, almost a secret hobby. Closing her eyes in various settings, she routinely navigated without light and taught each of her dogs to guide her in the dark by leaning against her knee. Recently, she learned to tie a hook on a line with her eyes closed, to tie it just right, just the way Mary Alice had taught her. In her forties, inspired by ergonomics textbook, she had invented an easy-to-use alternative to Braille—each letter was based on the standard Roman alphabet and framed by either a circle or square frame for easy identification and navigation. A public benefit corporation had improved the design extensively, to enhance tactile acuity.

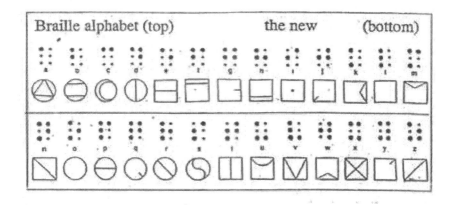

She listened, hoping that animals might rustle in the brush, and recalling how, when she went to the restroom, she often heard the single call of a wakened bird. If it was very dark, she might walk among those mysterious phosphorescent lights. Someone knocked on the wall. She didn't move. "We're going, to the north end, Libera. Feel free to join us. We have bait." It had to be Will or Mason. She didn't answer. She didn't even stir. She didn't want to go back to the beach or to attend the astronomy program.

The mosquitoes were killing them but most of the stargazers hung in there for the first hour, swatting and spraying, trying to get the constellations straight. The two oldest Nautilus boys, Waldo, and two coeds stood off to one side, not far from Fred. As the night grew darker, the Nautilus family ran out of bug spray and the coeds fled. More and more stars and planets appeared, but, by then, only a handful of campers remained on the beach with Ranger Bartholomew. He pointed out age-old legends and celestial navigation aids—Beetle Juice, Bellatrix, Cassiopeia, and Columbus' 26 degree latitude compass points and wonders of the universe. When Waldo drifted away, even before the moon rose, no one noticed.

By flashlight, Libera read Paul Bowles' *The Sheltering Sky*. When Kit was picked up by the camel caravan and the men shared her, Libera was aroused. Raising her nightie, she pretended that the fingers of her left hand were being licked and kissed; then she ran hands over her torso, toying, attentive, with all the time in the world, imagining the men's and her own pleasure, orchestrating and extending her rippling satisfaction. She turned off the light and reached inside the backpack, exploring and retrieving a little cotton pouch. This, at least for her, became better and better with age.

Chapter 6

Tuesday
February 3, 2016

Early that morning, with streaks of orange dawn still splashed across the sky, Libera fastened two buttons on her Worldwide Fisherman shirt, skipped coffee, and headed to the north beach with a bucket, rod, and thawed shrimp that wouldn't keep another day. Her breast pocket held a plastic pill jar with hooks and sinkers, and a rounded child's scissors was tied with an old shoelace to the handle of the five gallon bucket.

Someone had left piles of prime shells at the head of the path, but she didn't pause. She'd pick through them on the way back. At the end of the path, overlooking the rolling surf, a thin black man approached with long strides and long limbs: "No, no, Mama. You gotta get here earlier, first light, every day, every day. They was breakin' all over."

He grinned, showing several gold teeth. Maybe Bahamian, she thought. He might live in one of those private homes beyond the manatee lagoon. Maybe a caretaker, with the khaki trousers and the flapping work shirt, or his family may have come here generations ago on a merchant ship, or seeking shelter from a storm or from enslavement.

But why had early inhabitants left the settlement? When? Did a hurricane, disease, an attack, or some other calamity wipe them out? What secrets were buried here, what broken lives? It was difficult to imagine desperation and distress in such a beautiful place. She stood still and noticed a few swirls beyond the cusp of the waves, but the fish weren't still running. When she turned to talk, he was gone.

At the water's edge, black-bellied plovers scurried back and forth in unison, but the insouciant sandpipers strolled around and didn't seem to hunt. The sky was rose red, then pale rose, and then rose-blue as the hour passed. She cast, using shrimp and then a soft lure. She had forgotten the shovel again, so she dug for sand fleas with a cockle shell but the sand was too thin and she quickly hit a layer of broken shells. Where was the best spot to dig sand fleas on previous trips? She couldn't remember.

A great blue heron flew down twenty feet away and watched her. The wind lifted his feathered cowlick. He edged closer, hesitated, and then ate a shrimp that she tossed him. Within seconds, a flock of seagulls descended, squabbled over a second and third shrimp, and left again almost as quickly as they had come.

Years ago, she had often fished shoulder to shoulder with a great white heron in Key Largo, and she wasn't surprised when one appeared to her left. She tossed one shrimp after another to her. The larger blue heron squawked, flapped, and strode over in a fury. "OK, you eat first," she said. After that, in rapid succession, she tossed bait first to the right, and then to the left. Seagulls plummeted and scurried after the leftovers. It was such fun, like orchestrating paradise.

The fish weren't biting but Libera didn't care. Her biggest "strike" turned out to be an unopened beer bottle covered with barnacles, and she'd leave as soon as the shrimp were gone. The great white heron had a brilliant aquamarine triangle in front of her eyes, probably as camouflage for catching fish under water. How could such dazzling, singular beauty have evolved? What perfection!

Suddenly, Oscar appeared, running straight at the heron, driving her off.

"What the hell do you think you're doing?" Libera shouted, and threw handful after handful of sand at him.

"They eat the bait. Bold as brass," he snarled

"Get the hell out of here!" she yelled, and strode toward him.

He raised one hand in exasperation, puffed out air, and stalked away toward the dunes through deep sand—stiff-legged, resembling an irate, overweight stork.

When she returned to cabin 5, the charcoal wouldn't light, although it had been indoors overnight. Sand and salt had irritated the cut on her foot. Limping, gathering leaves and twigs from the ground, she wondered why several low-lying cocoa plum branches behind the cabin were bent and the ground beneath looked flattened, like an animal's bed. Libera wondered if a wild boar slept there. No squirrel or raccoon would flatten leaves that way. The leafy ground litter was damp from the heavy morning dew and useless as kindling, so she resorted to Sterno for coffee, resolving to collect wood for a roaring fire that night and live embers the next morning.

Relaxing on the porch, out of the corner of her eye, she noticed Oscar bustling outside cabin 7, diagonally across from 12. He'd be gone in two days. In the early rosy light, joggers padded by, singly and in groups. Three of the four girls on spring break ran by. Libera had forgotten that campers from the tent sites circulated freely among the cabins. The two brothers from Bangor ran past and nodded hello. Following a gung-ho muscular man, two bleary-eyed girls plodded by, mumbling to each other.

A completely Nike-outfitted woman trotted past by with a razor-thin prepubescent girl in tow: "Sweetie, please! Horses sweat, men perspire, men tingle."

Libera was hoping to get a glimpse of Fred Kenichi when a young couple ran by, arguing. "Why get rid of it? Selling it makes sense," panted the woman, tossing her long blond braid.

"Shut *up!*" Her partner hissed. "That lady on the porch with the luggage, *heard* you. *Now* what are we going to do?" They loped out of earshot.

Libera frowned. What could that girl be selling: illicit drugs, a baby, a gun? She heard the descending seven-note call of a cardinal, and then spotted him, flitting, blazing red in the hammock. By 9:00, the azure sky that Tuesday morning was simply beautiful. She couldn't wait to change cabins and go kayaking while the wind was so perfectly still.

Walking down the road, Fred surveyed Libera's bags and equipment scattered on the porch and ground in front of cabin 5. "Didn't you just arrive yesterday? I saw you leave the ferry at the landing," he explained.

"Um hum. And you were sketching. Now I remember."

"Calligraphy. I arrived Sunday. Are you leaving already? Is something wrong?"

She looked up at him. He seemed even more solid, more compelling than the night before. What a beautiful man, what an absolutely beautiful man. "I have to switch cabins. That's the way the reservation turned out," she said. "The tram will take me."

"May I help?"

"That would be so kind. I hate to have the tram man load all this by himself."

The two sat on the porch steps, waiting. He noticed the kayak paddle, net, and fishing rod resting against the wall next to a bucket with lures, bait, and canned soups. "I'm kayaking this afternoon," she said, pleased that this serene man hadn't asked about the cobbled gear.

The two gave each other a minimal account of their reasons for coming to Cayo Costa, and then sat quietly.

"May I see what you were writing?" she asked.

"I left the calligraphy set at the landing," he said. "I don't know what I was thinking. How's the foot?"

"I shouldn't walk much, so I'll kayak today after I move." She studied him. "And I'll fetch your set if it's still there."

"Let me see if I can suck out some of the spines," Fred said.

She could hardly breathe when he brushed the sand off her foot, moistened a clean handkerchief with his water bottle, cleaned the area, bent his head, and sucked. The pleasure was almost unbearable. And his magnificent bull neck was a sight she'd never forget.

On the mainland, in Coral Springs, Enid woke at first light and stuffed bottled water, a *Marie Claire* magazine, a towel, and a few clothes into the wet bag, including a bikini and a scanty Victoria Secret camisole. She couldn't wait to get out on the water. She slid the fifty-five pound Squall onto the car easily, even though she only weighed a hundred and ten pounds herself and was just a little bit of a thing. Nineteen and minimally endowed, she was often mistaken for a little girl. She tried to look older and sexier by wearing short shorts and skirts to show off her sensational legs, and risked orthopedically-incorrect stilettos and high espadrilles, even though she was a health nut.

The kayak's cockpit was too wide for her, a whopping 22 inches, but she had bought the boat used at a bargain price, complete with the paddle and spray skirt. A Current Design Slipstream was also on craigslist, a perfect fit, but it was too expensive, and red. She preferred yellow, to match the car, and hardly ever used hip braces anyway. And there was no time to wait for a perfect affordable kayak. She was in a hurry. At last, it was time to really live.

She knew Gilbert through the Blueway Paddlers Club. For the past two months, he had been buying fishing supplies in her father's hardware store, more than he needed. For some reason, Dad didn't take to him

Two weeks earlier, during the Tarpon Bay trip, Gilbert had confessed that he found her attractive and couldn't get her out of his mind. He was surprised how receptive she was, she could tell. She wanted to move fast. The Club had scheduled a Buck Key-Captiva trip for the end of the month, and she wanted everyone to notice that they were a couple. When he offered to share the cabin on Cayo Costa, she was thrilled. He presumed that she'd take the ferry, but she was determined to show off, kayaking from the mainland, maybe with rest stops on outlier islands, even though she had never kayaked any distance alone on open water. Either route to Cayo Costa, from Jewfish Creek or from Pineland Road, was longer than she had ever attempted solo but if she lost her nerve or if the weather turned foul, she could always change her plans and take the ferry from Jewfish Creek.

But what would Gilbert think if she took the ferry after Saturday morning's email? She had sent it right after checking the forecast. Tuesday's wind speed was supposed to be two to three miles per hour—not a following wind, but ideal otherwise. He'd be impressed if she paddled over. She wanted him to be proud of her, to take her seriously.

After stocking the shelves, Enid left her father alone in the store around 10:00. He thought that she was going kayaking on the Estero River with the Club, with two overnights on Mound Key. He hardly ever paid attention to her excursions; she could have made up any story, any one at all. The drive from Coral Springs to Jug Creek took an hour, so she might get out on the water well before noon. She had gone over and over the route from Jug Creek to Cayo Costa on PaddleSport charts, and would ask for advice at the marina. If there was time, she might stop on a sand spit and photograph birds, or stop at Cabbage Island to freshen up and buy a hamburger. And then, he'd be waiting for her at the landing. It might be the best day of her whole life.

Next to the loading platform at the fish plant, several customers and two workers watched her paddle out of Jug Creek by the back channel, waving goodbye. It was 11:30, a clear day, flatter than she could ever remember. The sun was to the northeast, over her left shoulder so there was no glare. As she paddled out of Jewfish Creek, she could clearly see Cayo Costa, but hugged the shore before venturing onto open water.

Then she sliced through a little chop on open water easily, as though she could paddle forever, but she skipped Cabbage Island. As she approached Cayo Costa, she noticed a lone figure leaning over the wharf's railing, staring into the water. Soon she'd be in Paradise.

In cabin 12 at last, Libera peeled a hardboiled egg. When she was young, the family's chickens and ducks gobbled shells up, maybe instinctively for hygienic reasons or for calcium. Thinking of chickens, she noticed a small board nailed to the door jamb on the outside of the women's toilet; it was identical to the chunk of unpainted wood that swiveled to lock the family's chicken coop years ago. But why lock a bathroom door on the outside? In case of a hurricane? And why were some ladies' restrooms on the right and some on the left?

Carrying fishing gear and her paddle, Libera locked cabin 12, tucked the key into her fins on the screened porch, and caught the tram to the landing. Sliding her boat out of the kayak rack, she stood for a moment and watched two tiny women land, climb out of a pair of sea kayaks, and head to the camp store. They appeared to be quite elderly. She wondered why the women wore long-sleeved shirts in the heat, and wide straw hats on open water rather than baseball caps.

Curious, she dragged the Keowee to the wrack line and studied their boats: two Wilderness Systems Tempests, one red and the other blue-green, with skegs. These were serious boats, with embedded compasses, and cockpits designed for athletic, narrow hips. Two tents were tucked into one bow's webbing, along with a camera and tripod. Evidently, the ladies never capsized. A Plano tackle box, collapsible rod, umbrella, and bedroll were tucked in the webbing of the other kayak. Presumably, food, clothing and water were in the wells.

She wished that they would come back before she left, so that she could meet them. Were they camping out there by themselves? Were they were professional photographers? She was puzzled that there appeared to be only one bed roll, but two tents. But she had to get going on the round trips to Pelican Bay, to the manatees, and back.

When she coasted into the channel and turned east into the bay, it was so calm that the reflection from both shorelines reached all the way to the boat —the sky, the mangroves, the anchored boats, and the beach. The mirrored effect almost gave her vertigo. Egrets and herons perched in the trees. How did that their dazzling white plumage protect them from predators? She felt privileged and strong, Tuesday's child, full of grace, grateful to be alive.

The wind was in the bay, but the current swept her back, southward, whenever she stopped to fish. And it didn't make any difference if she used thawed shrimp, squid, or lures, she hooked sea grass with nearly every cast. She caught and released a small red snapper. Then the line broke and she headed for the crescent shaped beach to tie on a leader and lure, and to rest.

On the strand, perched on driftwood, a solitary eagle watched her glide to shore. His head swiveled to watch the boats in the harbor, and then back to witness her clamber out of the kayak with difficulty, even though it was low tide. When the tide rose, it would be more arduous to scramble back into the cockpit; the bottom dropped off sharply at the high water mark. To her left, a tiny inlet led into an inviting lagoon, no more than a hundred feet away, but she decided to nap first. She pulled the Keowee on shore, climbed in, pulled her hat down over her face, and slept.

When the tram dropped Olivia off at cabin 5 a few minutes before 3:00, she exchanged pleasantries with Melony and Keisha, sitting in their screened porch next door. The two offered to help carry her ice, wood, backpacks, and cooler to her porch. "I'm in no hurry, thanks," she said, "Not here." That was the last contact she had with anyone on the island until morning. She fell into the bunk furthest from the door, Libera's old bunk. Asleep within minutes, she didn't hear a knock on the door an hour later, or the knocks after that.

Libera woke up refreshed and paddled into the adjacent lagoon. Startled mullet leapt in front and beside the Keowee, four to seven at a time. It was so off-the-wall, she had to laugh. "Jump in," she called. She had forgotten the drift anchor and had to paddle to the far shore periodically before the slight wind pushed her south again. The glorious herons and egrets, the secluded lagoon, and the leaping fish seemed magical. The mullet teased and frolicked, but didn't bite and not one jumped into the boat. She lost lure after lure in the rocks and sea grass on the bottom, but noticed pods of oysters attached to mangrove roots along the shore; it was easy pickings in the crystal clear water. She harvested a dozen for supper and with a good following wind, she kayaked effortlessly back toward the landing.

It was 3:15. She had to hurry if she wanted to check out the manatees and return to the landing for the 4:00 tram back to the cabin. "Just paddle a little past the landing and turn in," Ranger Tomás Hernandez had told her. "They're always there. We're worried. Two days ago, the naturalist noticed fresh gashes on one manatee's back, undoubtedly from a motor boat."

On the other side of the strand, sailboats and cabin cruisers sat at their moorings, still and quiet, except for the faint clank of the halyards. Beyond them, on the opposite shore, a houseboat, a huge sailing yacht, and several power boats also bobbed at anchor, facing the same direction as though choreographed. Where was everybody? She hadn't noticed any tenders at the landing and there wasn't an active boat in sight. She thought that she heard a few muffled voices, but perhaps not. Did people on the boats sleep during the day? What did they do all night?

Paddling abreast of the landing, she cut under the dock. No one was around; the 2:00 ferry had come and gone. As she rounded the corner, she noticed a yellow kayak overturned on the shore, jammed between a clump of mangroves and a moveable wharf. She paddled down the coast and entered a large lake on the right. Circling the periphery, since no manatees were in sight, she explored a small, shallow lagoon with a boarded-up house and a pier. She either sensed or saw a swirl, and then saw another. A large manatee circled, his contours difficult to see clearly against the dark bottom.

"Hey," she called to him. "Are you curious about me, too? Do you know that you are wonderful?" She heard an engine, froze, and buttoned her shirt. Within minutes, a cabin cruiser chugged into the lake, circled, and turned toward her. A dozen people were crowded into the cockpit, on the flying bridge, and on the bow.

"Is that one?" "Is that one over there?" Libera heard. She turned broadside and blocked the entrance to the shallow inlet. The boat motored up to her kayak and idled above her. Twenty-four eyes stared down at her.

"Listen. It's too shallow here for your boat. A manatee was slashed by a propeller, right here." No one answered. "Motor boats are not allowed. Turn back. Now," she ordered. She waited. "Now," she insisted.

The party boat reversed and circled the inlet twice more, perhaps waiting for her to go away, but she stayed until they left, feeling heroic. Good thing that she had worn tan shorts and a matching tan fishing shirt, she thought. She looked official.

She paddled back to the landing strenuously, cross-extensor, digging hard with one paddle while pushing forward all her might with the other, but the area was deserted. No tram. If only someone was there to help her, to sit on the bow and steady the kayak as she climbed out; but no one was in sight. Crunching onto the sand, she extracted herself little by little, taking her time, steadying the boat with the paddle across the coaming. Stiff and wet, she gathered the gear and paddle, thinking about the mile-long walk back to the cabin if she didn't catch a ride. But why had she rushed all day—rushing to fish that morning, rushing to see the manatees, and now rushing to catch the tram? Why worry? She had made her choices, had a grand day, and now could deal with it. Let it go. Deal with it. No problem. She grinned, taking her time. It was *her* life, after all. And it was lovely. Hers.

The yellow kayak was still wedged upside down in the mangroves—a Current Design Squall, an excellent boat. When the tide turned, the boat might lift and float away unless someone pulled it up above the wrack line. As tired as she was, she decided to haul it up, such a handsome craft, the poor thing.

Energized, she walked over to the Squall and lifted it a bit, with difficulty. Was it full of water? It couldn't be. She tipped the boat a little onto its rounded chines, but there wasn't enough room to flip it in the mangroves, so she pulled it backwards into the water, little by little, to overturn and float it. When the kayak rolled onto its side, she froze.

Hair waved in the water, like seaweed. Libera rocked the boat once, twice more, onto its keel. A woman's head bobbed in the cockpit, protruding through the opening of the spray skirt. Her mouth was open, shedding water.

Chapter 7

Homicide Detective Sergeant Gabriel Ortillo turned to Deputy Christie. "Murdered. Assaulted, pushed down into the cockpit, tipped, and forced under water. Bruises on the face, the eye probably gouged before death." They studied the grisly scene. The killer had stuffed the girl under the spray skirt, into the bottom of the cockpit, knees almost down to the foot braces. Only the head and neck were visible. In all probability, if Libera hadn't investigated, the inverted kayak would have stayed wedged between the trees and the beached dock until it lifted, tilted at high tide, and drifted into the channel.

Christie suggested, "This girl might not have struggled much. She couldn't use her arms." Gabe towered over her and standing next to his square, spare body, she felt comfortable, stronger. "Maybe the killer didn't have to be that strong, Chief."

"Uh huh. The lifejacket has a high collar. Old fashioned." Gabriel looked skyward. He growled, exhaling loudly as he often did when he was thinking, and nodded: "So maybe the killer couldn't get a grip on her neck, couldn't strangle her. So he pushed her down, held the top of her head, and rolled the boat until there was enough water to drown her."

Christie nodded. "Without that spray skirt, the poor kid might have been able to wriggle her way out when the kayak tipped."

Ortillo talked with his hands, his palms facing each other. "Big kayak, too big for this little girl, plenty of room, but the skirt created a death trap.

Sand and stones in her hair. He ground her face into the sand. Maybe 4 to 5 inches of water was all it would take. Very private, totally quiet. Could have surprised her, unexpected. And bending over a kayak, who'd notice him, who'd interfere?"

"That occurred to me, too. And the thing is, he had all the time in the world if he needed it—she couldn't cry out."

Ortillo plucked a strand of seaweed from his wrist. "Margery, there's no telling if she was killed before the ferry arrived or after—either way, it took only minutes. And no one on the ferry alerted anyone—no witnesses. Of course, arriving passengers might not notice rampaging elephants, they're so anxious to check in or get to a tram." He gestured in one direction and then another. "The day trippers rush to the beach to catch the rays, the campers hurry in the opposite direction to the office."

"And after waiting in the shelter on the other side of the pier, departing passengers rush straight to the ferry with the kids, luggage, and dogs. Boarding, they can't see this spot, no matter which way they face." Christie added, "I think someone on-island did this, somebody who knows the ferry schedules and the layout."

"We'll check out every camper who departed and those still renting, but departed day trippers will have to be tracked down on shore." Ortillo looked up at the kayak rack, about forty feet away. One shelf was empty, two rental boats were on the ground, Libera's was above the high tide mark. So, she'd taken the time to secure it, even after finding the body.

He groused. "But we'll never trace every public and private vessel that stopped here. Look at all these keel marks above the wrack line, Margery." He scratched his nose. He'd have footprints and other indentations photographed, but many more had been partially or entirely obliterated by his team and the incoming tide. And not only the murderer, but also unidentified kayakers, critical witnesses, might have left their boats below the wrack line because they were leaving soon. Their tracks were long gone.

He scoured the shoreline and the brush. Any arrivals, including the murderer, would notice immediately that the sandy cove was secluded where the kayaks put in—innocent kayakers might worry about someone stealing their boats and a murderer could allay his own set of concerns. Ortillo's gut told him that the killer probably was off-island if he paddled in and left by water. That's what he would do himself in that situation—unseen, or maybe noticed only by boaters who also had come and left. How to locate them? Receipts would show every kayak that came over on the ferry, but there would be no record of anyone who paddled in. Also, the killer might have taken a Boca Grande, Punta Gorda, Captiva, or Pine Island ferry over and left after the murder on whatever ferry landed next, paying cash, unrecorded. If so, that would indicate a local killer, from the mainland, counting on a timely exit and access to ground transportation at possibly more than one marina. There were many possibilities, suspects, and potential witnesses God-knows-where, but the most germane fact was that someone apparently waited for that girl and killed her quickly. Gabriel mulled over a possible motive; given the dearth of evidence, he had to start with the victim. Had she arrived on the island by chance or intent—was she planning to stay overnight? She had no tent, but lingerie. Who was she, what was she up to?

He paced back and forth, searching for her tiny boat-shoe footprints; but he didn't spot any, unless the rising tide had covered some, and he didn't think so. Libera's were easily-identifiable, one footprint deeper than the other because she limped. Many other barefoot and varied shod prints—including his, the deputies, and the rangers, were above the tide line. He stared at the high end yachts anchored off shore. A boat is a hole in the water into which you pour money, he thought. He pivoted, deep in thought, increasingly sure of one fact. That dead girl never got out of her kayak. Someone was waiting for her.

Christie gazed at the whistle on a lanyard around the victim's neck, rising and falling in the water, "Fassbender's the ME on duty, right? When will he get here? This case is on the evening news already. Someone called it in before we got here. Not that lady who turned the boat over, though. She's still up on that bench, showing her age a bit." She peered around the wharf, up at Libera and then down at her notes. "Came up Monday from Grassy Key. No phone."

Gabriel said, "There's poor cell reception, anyway. Maybe one of the boats out there in the harbor called it in. Let's hope that there were no photos. These damn smart phones, all these campers, you never know. Someone may have taken one already, before we came." Leaning forward and watching Libera, studying her, he continued. "Fassbender has a body off Colonial Boulevard so he'll do a quick preliminary there, before Forensics. He's all excited though, coming right over. He gets that way."

"She swears that the Squall wasn't there this morning," Margery said, nodding toward Libera. "Talked a lot about two old ladies, but the Ranger said those women were here early and stayed no longer than half an hour. I'd bet my bottom dollar that the killer's still around. We could get lucky if we get going here."

Gabriel made a moue, "All in good time." He cocked his head. "When she paddled back from Pelican Bay and passed by on the way to the manatees, would Dr. Grimaldi really have noticed the Squall so low in the water, on the other side of that floating pier? Maybe, maybe not."

"She'd notice a kayak. That's the one thing this lady wouldn't miss."

"We'll see. But she's probably right. It makes sense that the victim died earlier, right before she passed by, but after the Tropical Star ferry came and left. No rigor mortis when she was found. Lividity might be important. We shouldn't have any trouble with the time of death, but it won't help much."

"Don't you think it will be easy to find a killer on an island?" Christie suggested. She wished that they could move the poor kid's body to the beach. The area had been cordoned off, but evidence still had to be collected from the crime scene before the tide erased everything, minute by minute. Inside Libera's Keowee, above the wrack line, a bucket of oysters had tipped onto its side.

Up in the dark shelter, Libera sat and watched Ortillo and Christie, wishing that she could go down to them. She couldn't read her attending officer's nametag; the light was fading and her glasses were streaked. She should have cleaned the lenses when she used the rest room and she was stunned when the officer refused to let her go back for a tissue. How could this idiot think that she could be a flight risk? "That kayak was not there when I left this morning and it was when I passed by on the way to the manatees." she repeated. ""Please call Bucket about me," she added. "Detective James Buckman on Grassy Key. I know what I'm talking about."

"We will," Deputy Adrian Fitzhugh replied. "I told you that already, and you've asked me that twice before," he said in exasperation, wishing he was at the murder scene and not lady-sitting with this old bat, watching her lose it. Or maybe she had lost it a long time ago. Maybe she was the killer. There was something nasty about her—too damn sure of everything. Bossy. "Bucket, bucket, bucket." She sounded like that scene from Monty Python, the one with the glutton eating everything in sight—"Bring me a bucket." At least she wasn't asking for a lawyer, like most of them. He'd love to handcuff her to the bench and go hear what the Chief was saying.

He gave Libera a withering look, left his post, and went to brief the Chief about Detective Buckman. What a bully, Libera thought, watching him walk down to the beach. I hope he isn't married. I hope that he has no children. I hope he never will. I hope he's not happy. I hope he can't sleep nights.

The Chief saw Adrian coming. That guy never does what he's told, he thought. How hard would it be for him to wait up there, and obey orders? But Ortillo listened patiently and said, "Officer Fitzhugh, I'll give

Homicide Detective Jimmy Buckman a call down in Marathon tomorrow night, when we've sorted this out a bit. You just go back to the shelter up there with Dr. Grimaldi, and stay put."

"As long as he knows whose case it is," interrupted Adrian, puffed out his cheeks, thinking that it was pretentious for Libera to call herself "doctor" when probably she only had a Ph.D.—no matter how important she may have been once. He was sick of old people who put on airs.

"I'll call him. Hey, if he can help out, even just get her to relax and recreate this afternoon's events, that would be great. And maybe, just maybe, this case is connected to the murders he had down in the Keys last year. You never know." I want to have more to go on by the time he comes, Gabriel thought; it won't hurt to wait another day or two before calling.

Abruptly, Gabriel waved Adrian away. "I'm going to walk around, get the feel of the place. Tell Dr. Grimaldi I'll chat with her later, at her cabin." He looked forward to talking with Libera, lingering, letting her talk, getting to know her. Her composure and manner of speaking fascinated him. He couldn't help it. What the hell. Why not?

He turned to Christie, "Get me a matrix of all the ferry schedules, please. Let's hope that no day tripper from Punta Gorda or Captiva paid cash, pulled this off, turned around, and then took a different ferry back, to get off Cayo Costa quickly. Give that some thought, Margery, but let's concentrate on the Bokeelia boat for now. How many campers came in today? Sixty passengers came in; teams on shore will have to try and track down the forty-three who left," Gabriel mused.

"Some of those who departed may have been day trippers or campers from a variety of earlier passages," Christie added. "Not to mention the boaters, shell-seekers, employees, and service people coming and going to and from the park irregularly, during all sorts of unscheduled. She might as well have been killed in Grand Central."

"But if the crime was premeditated, and it sure as hell looks like it, the suspect must have come here and waited around, right here, right before the assault. And that points to the Bokeelia passage. Probably long after the old ladies left and shortly before Libera happened to kayak by," Gabriel said. "But we'd like to find the two ladies and ask if they noticed anyone lingering or an overturned kayak. They should be easy to find and I'll bet you that the Squall wasn't here yet then."

"We'll work on it. We have the Coast Guard."

"One problem—we have little information on the tent folk who paid cash on the ferry," Gabriel said. "Except through license plate numbers if they parked at a marina." We've got our work cut out for us here, he thought.

"Don't campers have to show IDs when they check-in though, to be assigned a site or a cabin?" Christie asked. "Don't we have that, at least?"

"Not everyone in a tent does, just one person." Ortillo sighed. "Check what information Edwards and the ferries can provide. Let's presume that the drivers' licenses are valid. Credit card information is critical because we have little else to go on, unless someone paid for parking. There's only one thing I know for certain, Margery. That nice lady up there with Adrian can't be a person of interest."

Christie raised her eyebrows and paused, before asking, "What if someone paddled over from Pineland Road?"

"Well, that is the quickest route, better than Jug Creek, and everybody knows it. But there's no parking on Pineland after sunset. The department checks the cars at dusk, and then sends the tow truck out. The timing might be tight. Wouldn't it be risky to paddle out, wait in ambush between 2:00 and 3:30, drown the victim when no one's around, and kayak back before dark—with no one noticing you or your boat here on shore? Or someone could have kayaked over from Cabbage Island." We're going in circles, he thought, growling. But that will change.

Adrian rushed down to Gabriel. "The Pine Island police called, Chief. Both the lady in the Chandlery at Jug Creek and the men in the fish plant remember the victim because she had the pricey Squall, asked directions, and left her keys when she paid for parking. They traced her license plate, registration, address, and credit card number and the car is registered to one Enid Somers. More information is coming in. Ranger Edwards says she had no reservation here."

"Why the lingerie, then?" Christie asked. "Why no tent or sleeping bag? Where did the victim plan to sleep tonight? Isn't that critical?"

Gabriel broke in. "You're right. Ask them to get over to her house, question the neighbors, and find where she worked. We need a robust file on this lady within 24 hours—to establish a motive, ASAP. I can't keep these people here much longer. I hope to God they're shipping enough food, water, and paper products over."

Adrian lingered. "That Grimaldi lady has a stubborn streak. And she's mean." He pursed his lips and nodded. "I think she did it. She's the one."

"Drop it. Now. A boatload of tourists saw her at the manatee lagoon." That guy has a problem with women, Gabriel thought. Perspiring, licking the salt from his lips, he wished that Fitzhugh had brought bottled water down and less lip. "Deputy Christie, drive Dr. Grimaldi back to her cabin. There's no need for her to sit through the 6:00 interrogations with the other campers."

"She looks beat." Christie nodded. "Says she has no family close by. She couldn't remember her license plate number, by the way."

Gabriel turned away. "Is that a fact." He stood stock still, staring at the crime scene, at the Squall and the shoreline, memorizing details. More help had arrived at the landing. Forensics, the medical examiner, rangers, and detectives bustled about and headed toward him from the docks and the shelter. But he remained immobile.

Fred was also immobile, watching, hidden in the trees next to the path leading from the mullets' lagoon. Where were they taking Libera? He toyed with the idea of borrowing one of the boats moored near the wharf if she needed an escape.

And Mia and Roger Templeton, together with Sasha and Stas Rodzianko, watched Fred from *their* hiding place behind the bike rack. "Don't tell anybody about him yet," Mia whispered. "We want to catch him red-handed." Wolf watched a flutter of movement on an anchored cabin cruiser offshore.

The mate on that boat glanced at the action around the yellow kayak now and then, while he sewed hooks into frozen mullet for the next day's tarpon fishing, in case they ran out of live pinfish or if shrimp weren't working.

And in a bobbing skiff tied to the far dock, Sebby and Morgan hid under a canvas and watched Ortillo, wondering how to wade to shore unnoticed. Morgan was nervous. "Pops won't even miss us," Sebby reassured him.

"And that's important? Why? He wouldn't miss us if we were lying in the road in front of the tram, he's so bogus. The main thing now is, how to get out of this boat without any of these guys seeing us, you dwork. Hiding here was so lame."

"It wasn't my fault. The park locks their paddles inside the cage, so I borrowed those two from the dock. How did I know that they would load those kayaks onto the ferry before we got back?" He dug his fingernails into his arm until it hurt. "They're going to be really, really pissed when they notice they're missing." Sebby's whisper was too loud. "When they find the paddles here, let's not tell them a thing. Not about what we've been doing, not about anything we saw, nothing. If we mention anything at all, they'll never leave us alone. We don't have to tell them anything."

"That's the first smart thing you've had to say all week, but don't keep saying it," Morgan ordered.

"And what about the calligraphy set that we found at the landing this afternoon? The Jiggler, that guy with the bouncing knee, was sitting near there. Maybe he'll tell on us. "

"Naah. That can be our little secret, too," Morgan mumbled. "I have to take a leak. So maybe we should just climb out, drop into the water, and walk to shore like kids looking for crabs."

"Without a net?" Sebby asked. "Won't it look funny?"

"Kids might try to catch crabs without a net. They do that sort of thing."

"Not at high tide."

The crime perimeter had been set up, Christie had dropped Libera off at cabin 12, and the rangers and the staff were instructing campers to assemble in the pavilion near cabin 1—those they could find. Ranger Edwards told Molly, "Thank God the wedding party left first thing this morning."

"But they rented two private homes, right?"

"Still, we would have had to question them. As it is, locating everyone this afternoon is a problem, and keeping them here any length of time is impossible. Did you notice that the Russian kids now hang out with the wolfhound kids. Those four are up to something. They claim that they have to walk that damn dog again, and lo and behold, their little gang keeps turning up all over the place. The big sister, Mia, is the ring leader. Just do your best." He tapped a pencil on the railing. "They might think this murder investigation is some sort of game. Maybe you can get a look at their little notebook to see what they're up to.

"According to Esme," Molly said, "most campers aren't at the tent sites or cabins at this hour. She only found one old fellow reading on the porch at cabin 1, cabin 8 was drinking on his porch, and the two professors going at it in cabin 2; but no one answered at cabins 3, 4, 5, 7, 9, 10, 11, or 12. Cabin 9's door was ajar, so she nudged it and peeked in—it looked like the two backpacks inside hadn't even been unpacked—that's it. "

"Going at it?"

"Arguing. Not sure about what, and no one else was within earshot. Almost everyone is still fishing or biking or searching for shells before sunset. Cabins 3 and 10 look deserted. Some woman from the ferry checked into 5 but no one came to the door."

"We keep hearing about a massive man who checked into 9 on Monday. Asian? Scaring the kid in the shower? When are we actually going to meet this phenomenon?"

Jonathan said, "We might want to check the backpacks in there if no one shows up. Keep everyone way from the landing, is all. Send them to the pavilion near cabin 1. Tomás is checking the beach. Esme is covering the tents. Hopefully, everyone will turn up before dark."

"Or not, the way this day has been going," she said.

Detective Ortillo commandeered a tram and drove to see Libera. If he stayed at the landing, they'd bother him with one thing after another, he rationalized. He was surprised that he was a little nervous about calling on her. He hoped that she wouldn't mind; there wasn't any way he could have called first. Anyway, if she was sleeping, it was better to pop over there unannounced. While she was waiting at the landing, they'd checked her vital signs and given her a sedative. But maybe she was awake, the type to shun pills.

Libera was sitting on the screened porch in fresh clothes, writing. When he walked over, she waved him in and looked around, as if she was surprised that there was only one chair. He was edgy when she suggested that they sit inside, and was relieved when they walked in and she said, "It's a mess in here. I never unpacked when they moved me from cabin 5. There's a table outside."

Backing out, Gabriel noticed two loaves of bread, dish towels, sandals, and two books in an open duffle bag. Toiletries spilled out of a backpack. On the little corner shelf, he noticed a toothbrush, 3 cans of Sterno, two flashlights, half a candy bar, and a fishing reel. The lady was a free spirit.

At the picnic table, she stopped and turned. "What do you think?" Gabriel didn't have a chance to answer. "That kayak was way too big for her, you know. Was there food or extra clothing in the well? Were there any books? Did she have blisters or did she wear kayak gloves?" Libera lowered herself onto the bench, gripping the edge of the table.

"Are you hurt?" Gabriel asked.

"Just stiff. Always," she replied. "Plus, I stepped on a sea urchin last night and have no idea where the Aleve is." She raised her eyebrows, paused, reached into a breast pocket, and scraped a dented pill capsule out—the sedative. He couldn't help noticing that she had only fastened two buttons. He couldn't help glimpsing more.

"The sedative?" he asked.

She nodded. "Never touch them."

"Why did you visit Cayo Costa?" he asked.

"To relax, get my act together. I come often, keeps me sane. But this time, I'm not sure that I should have come."

He nodded.

"Are they going to impound the Keowee?" she asked. When he pursed his lips, she pressed him: "I'm talking about my Keowee kayak." In the silence, she looked into his eyes, his beguiling dark eyes. "Want a drink? I have grapefruit Crystal light—hard to come by nowadays."

Even though he hated anything grapefruit and all powdered drinks, he nodded. While she limped inside and returned with two paper cups, he tried to think of something to say. He'd better ask her *something*. She was doing all the talking.

He sipped the drink, having no idea that she had retrieved those grapefruit packets on a trash picking foray on Grassy Key, that she routinely hunted for discarded treasures as a matter of course, and that she was serving him the drink even though the canister's expiration date read 2001. Sitting there near her, was he overwhelmed, relaxing, or absorbing facts? Had he said anything at all? Had he been daydreaming or had he said something—maybe about the drink? He wasn't sure.

She chatted. "On the ground here at night, in the open, you sometimes see shining green dots. I think they might be phosphorescent insect eyes." Then she became silent, unmoving, staring at a crow flitting through the branches of the beach plum above them. She appeared to have run out of steam too.

They sat together without talking, comfortable in the silence. He could see that she was worn out.

Then he rose. "We're gathering all the kayaks, not just yours," he told her. "So no one can paddle away." He nodded toward the road. "I'll be in cabin 3 tonight, all night. Just knock."

She smiled. She thought he was a hunk and surprised herself when she asked "Does your wife know how long you'll be here?"

"Not married. You?" he asked, not surprised at all. She shook her head, unable to hide a slight grin.

"Ravioli?" she asked.

He shook his head. "Try to behave yourself," he chortled. Then he added, "Be careful, Libera dear. I'll wait until you're back on your porch."

Driving back to the pavilion, he muttered, "Get serious, damn it! What the hell's the matter with you, Gabe? This is serious!" He thought that he should slap himself on the forehead, at least twice. But he was grinning, smitten.

Chapter 8

Gabriel had requested extensive land-based support, real time communi-
cations, and instant background information, but he didn't want anyone to show up and bother him yet, not while he reviewed and reviewed
his initial impression of the girl in the kayak. He had to think. Had he
missed something—an item out of place, a detail that didn't fit the site or
the moment of the murder?

That late afternoon, time alone was essential. He wanted to think, by
himself, and let his team and the park personnel take care of the bunch
of Walden Pond wannabees. His officers, the rangers, and the staff had
rounded up most of the campers by 6:30, but there were stragglers here and
there who could not be collected until after sunset—all in good time. After
all, the only one leaving the island was the victim.

At the pavilion, the Nautilus family helped to set up a table and lan-
terns, and Ranger Esme White handed Deputy Christie a list of tenters,
cabin people, registration information, and the campground schema.
"Cabins 3 and 10 are empty, Dr. Grimaldi is in 12, and we didn't find
anyone at Cabins 5, 6, 7, or 8, but most of them may be here already. I'll
check that, right now."

On shore, the local sheriff and police departments were looking into
Enid's background and interrogating day trippers. All ferries would be
pressed into delivering supplies and personnel. The Coast Guard had closed
the harbor; most boats at anchor were unoccupied anyway. Everyone kept

an eye open for the two elderly women in the Wilderness Systems kayaks, to warn them. It still hadn't occurred to anyone that they might be killers.

In the pavilion, Phil asked, "Where's Sebby?"

Morgan slid down the bench in front of him, towards the coeds, and replied, "Not here. He couldn't keep up."

Phil picked up *Boat Goat* and resumed reading. Sebby arrived, breathless, plopped down, and leaned against his grandfather. "Does this mean we get to stay longer, Pops?"

"Time will tell," Phil murmured, turning a page, not looking up. Sebby sat up straight.

"Are you apprehensive, Pops? Because of the murder?" Morgan asked. He made a resolution to use the word "trepidation" soon. He liked the sound of "discombobulated" also.

"Haven't given it much thought," Phil replied. "Who would want to kill me? Just be careful. Stick together. Do you need money, boys?"

"We could use some," Morgan told him. "Here are the drinks and snacks you asked for, but I couldn't find your other book anywhere."

"I have it," Phil said. "Had it right here, all along."

The crowd buzzed about the little girl who had drowned. Gilbert listened, presuming that Enid had heard about the tragedy and decided not to come or wasn't allowed to land. He would have been pleased if she hadn't shown up for any reason. He didn't need the hassle.

Ranger Esme White strolled through the tent ground again and again with a bullhorn, telling campers to gather at the pavilion. One camper reported, slipped away because nothing was happening, and returned to site 30, right next to the Cabin Trail, to unpack his gear before dark. When he heard chatter at the junction, he strolled over with the frying pan still in his hand and listened to snatches of a conversation about a girl's body in a kayak at the landing. He slapped the pan against his thigh, twice, and returned to the tent. He had to act soon, and he didn't have a plan.

Deputy Christie and Ranger Edwards scanned the registration and passenger lists. They asked campers about their whereabouts that afternoon and what they had heard and seen, not *whether* they had heard or seen anything. A bare-bones collage of almost everyone's activities emerged. Melony and Keisha had collected shells all morning, heated lunch, relaxed on their porch, and saw Gilbert, the real estate agent, carrying a rod and a tackle box when he returned to cabin 8 around 1:00 and sat on his porch, drinking beer. The elderly gentleman in cabin 1 read on the porch—all day, as far as they could tell. The five Russians were in and out cabin 11, together, until their boys joined the Templeton children around 2:00, walking the dog. After a late lunch, Mary and Spencer walked the short distance to the wildlife posters and exhibits next to the beach path. The professors vouched for several tenters in that area from 2:30 to 3:00, and noticed Mason and Will leave cabin 6 around 3:30, probably to fish the north beach on the tide. No one had seen anyone around cabin 9 or 10 all morning. When asked, Mary, an early riser, stated that she didn't see the Asian gentleman at all that morning.

As she turned away from Deputy Christie, Mary was relieved to see Morgan show up, and then Sebby. She hadn't seen the boys all day, and eavesdropped when Morgan dragged Sebby aside before he was questioned. Leaning over the edge of her bench, she heard him remind the little boy to shut up about a boat and paddles. She made up her mind to ask Morgan what was going on as soon as she had a chance, but not to tell anyone else.

The benches had no backs, and campers bent and twisted to see their fellow captives, reserved initially, but chatting as time passed. Some older campers were clearly uncomfortable on the benches and Christie wondered why Adrian interviewed Gilbert first. Did Adrian find it easier to relate to a man close to his own age? She listened critically, wondering why his questions lacked substance.

"Why did you come to Cayo Costa?"

"To fish. I reserved cabin 8 a month ago and then came earlier because of a cancellation. I always take a break at this time of year. You could check. Home sales are pretty slack in February."

"What's your line of work?"

"Real estate—Coral Treasures."

"Did you know any of the other campers before you came?

"No."

"Did you catch any fish today, see anything unusual?"

"Three snook in the mangroves. I was going to grill them tonight," he said, palms upward. "Didn't see a thing."

"OK. That's enough for now. We'll have more to discuss tomorrow."

"Probably they already know who did it," Phil said, to no one in particular. "This could be a waste of time." He nodded at Ortillo and then at the road. "Around 5:00, that detective drove past with Libera, that woman in cabin 5, the kayaker."

Spencer added, "Probably the Sheriff is holding her."

A man sitting directly behind Spencer couldn't stop tapping his leg. Sebby whispered to Morgan: "Jiggler, Gray Man, Fatso, and Bogus are here, but no Odd Job,." Morgan punched him in the arm.

The Virginia coeds braided cornrows in each other's hair, undid them, and braided them again. Gilbert thought that the four of them lined up like that looked stunning.

Gabriel nodded to Adrian and the rangers, put his pen in his chest pocket and announced, "All campers must remain on the island until we discover more about the murder."

"Murder? I thought that a little girl drowned kayaking," Gilbert said.

Gabriel wondered where this guy been all that day, meditating? "It doesn't look that way," he said. "That'll be all for now."

Rangers White and Hernandez made sure that everyone returned to their cabins or tent sites without incident. In addition to quarters in cabin 3, Ortillo had cabin 10 at his disposal since the women with all the children had left on Tuesday, a day early, for some reason. He knew that he wouldn't need it until reinforcements arrived tomorrow, but he thought how refreshing it would be to stick Adrian in there—all alone, all night, in the dark.

Campers straggled back to the cabins and tents. Only a few had flashlights since they had assembled while it was still light. The moon had not yet risen. No one lit a fire ring that night, and only four or five fishermen went surf casting. Inside cabin 12, Libera wrote for hours. Cayo Costa was quiet and still.

Chapter 9

Since Olivia hadn't slept well and rose at 4:00 that morning in Sanibel, to check her files and emails, she was exhausted when she boarded the ferry. By the time she reached Cayo Costa, she thought that she could sleep for days, and chortled when she faced the rows of bunks in cabin 5, all for her. Climbing into the far bunk in the right corner, the same bunk that Libera had slept in the night before, she felt insulated, isolated, fresh, and innocent: I am still, at rest now. I am and will be at rest. I am whole. That is why I came here. Within minutes, she was asleep—an island upon an island.

When she awoke and went to the restroom to freshen up and wash her underwear at the outside spigot, it seemed odd that no one was around. Maybe there was a performance at the pavilion. It was quiet and still and, had she been lucky, it wouldn't have mattered a bit that she knew nothing about the body, the investigation, or the interrogations. And it wouldn't have mattered that she also slept through the commotion at the restroom that evening.

"Some redneck locked me in the damn toilet over there. The Ladies Room next to cabin 12," Melony told Keisha when she returned to cabin 4.

"Who did? You're kidding, right?"

"No. I'm not. I kicked and pounded and yelled, and he let me out. One of those boozers in cabin 6. He whined that *he* didn't do it. I got his name—Mason."

"Why would he do that, after all we've been through at the pavilion?"

"That's what *he* said, too. Who knows?"

"Why is there a lock on the outside of the bathroom door, anyway?"

"Maybe he put it there."

Shortly before dawn, Olivia woke but didn't move, reliving a painful memory: "You come back here. Don't you dare run! Don't you dare! When I get finished with you, you'll wish you were never born." She sat up and hit her head on the upper bunk. There it was again—not a nightmare, not a dream in a half-awake state, but that vivid memory—cornered in the attic again. She had always tried to make herself scarce in the late afternoon, before the boys and her sisters came home, before Dad finished at the office, after the housekeeper went home—that was the danger hour, when she was the only one there and Mom was restless.

For over forty years, what mattered to her, what she never knew, was—did anyone else know what was going on? Whose decision was it to send her away to a convent boarding school during the school year, to camp in the summer, and to live with an aunt when she was older?

"We never had a bit of trouble with Olivia," her mother used to say. "She was the easiest of all the children." After her death, when her brothers mentioned that Mom had never laid a hand on any of them, Olivia finally understood. That's where poems had come from, and the love of research, from the arms-length life of a girl who preferred not to be touched, who turned away from the love of her life and married someone safer.

At fifty, too busy perhaps, but content and successful, she finally under-stood how lucky she was to escape that home as soon as possible and to be men-tored by an army of surrogates who believed in her. They were all gone and she was on her own, and she had never thanked those women enough. Last month, waiting for a flight at the Providence airport, her old home town, she realized that she might be sitting right next to classmates, friends, and teach-ers from Elmhurst, her beloved alma mater; or across from neighbors whom she had once knew well, before she went into exile. But so many decades had passed, she might not recognize them, and none of them probably knew who she was, either. Visible but unrecognizable, she was a ghost among ghosts.

But not on Cayo Costa. There she was alive, in the moment, and truly authentic. It was perfect, absolutely perfect, this place waiting for her, expecting her return, still there. And Cayo Costa hadn't changed at all. In fact, it was better, because she was better, more complete with age.

The night was still and clear and silent when she walked out onto the porch. Descending the cabin's steps, she studied the sky, motionless, until she heard a mosquito. As she stepped away from the cabin with her soap, towel, and toothbrush, she heard a chirp or a cluck No embers glowed in the fire rings at either cabins 4 or 6.

She tried to remember the name of the solitary planet beneath the moon as she walked. She didn't need a flashlight. In the moonlight, the road was clearly visible—a mystical silver gray. At the edge of the beach path, across from cabin 6, Olivia noticed a big white shape, like a shroud, about fifteen feet high. Curious, she shuffled closer and realized that it had to be an old dead tree, towering and silvered in the moonlit brush.

Approaching the restroom, she saw reflective signs, *Men* and *Women*, on the left and the right, respectively, yet back at the landing, the men's was on the right and the women's on the left. Everyone must think that's odd, she thought. The moonlight shone through the skylight into the stall—peaceful, elemental. Everyone was asleep—she had missed them again, it seemed. On the way back to the cabin, she stared at the white tree again. It looked like a sheet or a ghost, very Macbeth. What special quality made the wood appear white in the dark? She left the road and again walked to a few feet of the pale object—just a dead tree, but what an apparition. Strange—why had the park left it there—as a home for raccoons or owls or a lair for a rare specimen? She would take a closer look in the morning, before she joined Ranger Esme White's flora and fauna tour. That week, she had all the time she wanted to do whatever she liked.

Turning away, she returned to the cabin. She had left it unlocked; a key was a bother in the dark. She hardly had fallen asleep again when she woke up coughing. Alert, she rushed to the door, but it was jammed from the outside. She flung herself against one window screen and then another and bruised herself on closed, fastened shutters. Why were the shutters closed? Who had locked them?

Dropping to the patch of floor that was hot but not ablaze, scorching her hands, she crawled to the door, peering beneath it, trying to see what was blocking it. She didn't have a tool, the time, or the breath to push the obstacle away. How could it be that no one else heard, saw, or scented what was going on? She'd be dead in a few minutes. Just a few minutes. It wouldn't hurt any more.

The noise of was deafening—*ka-puck, ka-puck, ka-puck*—definitely a helicopter. Libera sat up, rolled over, rushed to the door, and saw flames across the road to the left, lighting the interiors of cabin 6 and 4. And there was no mistake about it, somewhere down the beach path was a helicopter. Landing? Taking off?

Through the trees, she could see that cabin 5 was on fire. Could she have left something burning there yesterday morning? Smoke was blowing her way, her eyes smarted, and ashes rained down on the path. Could sparks from a fire ring have spread and caused such an intense blaze? That previous morning, not only the charcoal was damp, but also dead leaves and loose sticks around that cabin wouldn't ignite, no matter how hard she tried; she had needed Sterno for her coffee. Someone else must have been careless. She hadn't noticed who checked into cabin 5 yesterday but recalled that someone did have a reservation. Probably someone careless, she thought. Were they safe?

Two trams, a truck, and the Rangers' Club car were parked on the road in front of 5 and between the cabins. Ranger Edwards and White, the staffer Molly Standish, and an army of volunteers fought the fire with extinguishers and water from the restroom's outdoor sink. At the best of times, campers are a rag tag group, but that morning, in various stages of dress and undress, the crowd resembled the out-patient clinic from an insane asylum, and yet the ash-covered and coughing volunteers formed an efficient bucket brigade. Libera recognized Melony and Keisha, the Rodzianko boys, and Mia and Roger Templeton in front of the sink, passing containers of water to the motley chain, many wearing sleepwear. Her bucket was missing from the picnic table bench. They must have borrowed it. Where was Gabriel?

How could she have slept through this melee? How embarrassing. Tuesday's mayhem must have exhausted her. It was hot, the smoke hurt her eyes, and she couldn't stay there, upwind, so she put on sandals and a fresh pair of shorts, buttoned one button, grabbed a hat, and headed up the cabin road toward the harbor. She forgot to bring a water bottle, she was in such a hurry to leave. The melee was too much for her. She was in the way, anyway.

Since the firefighters had commandeered both sides of the loop, she skirted the crowd and the vehicles, walking into the prairie behind the cabins and then back to the road. No one noticed her. At the facilities across from cabin 1, leaning on the railing of the handicapped ramp, she paused, deciding what to do. Soon the sun would rise; it was already light enough to see. She was only wearing sandals and her foot hardly hurt at all, so she decided to walk to the landing and rent a bike; that way, she wouldn't be on her feet all morning. She had no money or water, and it never occurred to her to return to the cabin to get some, not when she just wanted to get out of there and be alone. That burned smell would last for days, possibly weeks. Not one bird sang. "I'm out of here," she mumbled. "They don't need me in the way," she reiterated.

On the main road, relaxing in the increasing light, detached, Libera folded herself into the island, the scrub and then the forest. She had waited almost a year to explore Cayo Costa again, to be free. She stopped thinking about the fire, child-like, compartmentalizing at will, when she found a metal bottle cap. Wouldn't that be invaluable, a fine scraper, a treasure if she were marooned on a desert island? Walking past a wooded area, she studied a trench at the edge of the hammock, hoping to find a wild pig's hoof prints, or perhaps to see or hear the animal himself. Roadside, birds now tittered in the growing light, morning glories climbed up cocoa plum trees. She was surprised that there was sufficient sunlight for blossoms in the dense shade. Not one jeep, tram, or emergency vehicle drove by. They were probably all fighting the fire, she remembered. She had forgotten about that.

For some reason, a chainsaw crew had radically trimmed the palmettos along the road and cut down cabbage palms; traces of their trunks were still in the sand, and scorching in the dense hammock suggested controlled burning. She was surprised that she hadn't seen raccoon tracks anywhere. Occasionally, she passed a bench but she didn't rest. She drifted along as though on autopilot., deeper into the dark forest road, and it was silent. Spanish moss, almost uniformly brown, and vines, including poison ivy, added to the dense shade and made it difficult to see through the trees. Were those two mud puddles not far off the track caused by rooting animals?

Suddenly, headed right for her, a tall and skinny man on a yellow rented bicycle surprised her. She hadn't heard him coming. He roared with laughter as he sped past, and then started singing *O Solo Mio*. She didn't think it strange. It was an excellent day to cycle too, to gather her wits about her.

The shop didn't open until 9:00 at the landing, and she had forgotten money anyway. She'd pay later. She didn't have to remember every little thing, anyway, not when she was so free. To spare her knees, she chose the bicycle with the highest seat and peddled back up the Cabin Trail toward the cemetery. When she registered, Ranger Edwards had given her maps of both the campground and the trails with the key, but, anxious not to keep the tram waiting, she hadn't even glanced at either of them and the maps were in the laundry by now, in her other shorts. Without water, she couldn't bicycle in the heat for much more than an hour anyway.

Only she would be this careless—why hadn't she at least taken the water bottle from her kayak or taken a moment to drink from the bubbler at the landing? If she could just find the Pioneer Cemetery, she'd double back and get her act together, right away. But at the first fork, she absently turned left and biked along a rough stretch that seemed too long, and then took a right, presuming that it would lead to either the Gulf or Quarantine Trail. Surely, sticking to the coastal trails and circling, it would be impossible to get lost. And there might maps posted somewhere on the main trails. She wondered, if Fred Kenichi was looking for her, if she shouldn't head back to the cabins and forget the cemetery. But she had no idea where she was.

"Not an accident, not at all. Smell that accelerant? If traces are on the arsonist, we'll nail him." Gabriel wanted to curse. "That poor woman was almost burned like a witch, would never have crawled out, if it weren't for that skinny kid who saw flames and pulled the wedge away from her door. What the hell with that wedge?"

"The kid looks just like that cartoon character Waldo," Adrian interrupted.

"Jefferson Davis Tate," Margery Christie said. "Claims he's fifteen—'a runt' he called himself. Says his parents were making noise." She looked at her notes. "Says he went out to see Cassiopeia."

"On the road? Not on the beach, not in the open where he could actually see the entire sky? At five in the morning?" Gabriel asked. "Is one of the coeds, by chance, named Cassiopeia?"

"Can we hold him?" Adrian asked.

"Don't be an ass." Gabriel peered at Margery's notes. "No sign of accelerant on him. So the kid wanders, so what. The Nautilus family verified that he was at the star gazing, asking questions, on Monday, and one coed insists that she heard his parents' ruckus Tuesday night."

"'Yowling,'" she told me." Margery smirked. "'It sounded like a cat yowling.'"

"But she might be lying," Gabriel cautioned.

"Why?" Adrian asked.

"A horny fifteen year-old and a shy nineteen year-old?" Gabriel smiled. "Do the math. We probably know what he had in mind. But not why he ended up here, alone." He scuffed a half circle in the sand. "What the hell—after the dead girl yesterday—what's tying all this together, what did those two women have in common? What went on last night? Gather everyone in the pavilion again, by 2:00."

"Olivia Longo is a famous geneticist, Chief," Christie volunteered. "The department sent over a synopsis of her research. There might be an issue there, saving or manipulating fetal tissue, something like that. Someone stalking her? Anyway, she's the mother of four college-age children, including one set of twins—a litter. The two women in cabin 4 met her around 3:00, and she seemed fine, happy." Margery frowned: "But what if we don't find a connection with the kayaker, Enid Somers?"

Gabriel shrugged. "And what do we know about *her?*"

"Not much. Enid was just a local shop girl who worked in her father's store."

"Husbands?" he asked. "Boyfriends? Had the two women ever met?"

Margery shook her head. "Olivia arrived from Sanibel yesterday; her husband is in Iceland for four months, on a grant. She reserved the cabin a long time ago." She paused. "But Enid was single, with no reservation, carried only a magazine and minimal clothing in the kayak's wells—some interesting lingerie, by the way."

"The same murderer, just a different method? It's a stretch to imagine two killers in this limited area, this short time. And it's hard to believe that there wasn't some link between those women," Gabriel said. "It wasn't as though each was in the wrong place at the wrong time. There's intent here, on both the victims' and the killer's part. And method." He pulled at an ear. "Not to mention unlimited access, when you think about it." He growled.

Over Deputy Christie's shoulder, Adrian mumbled, "The victims probably never met." He tilted his head dramatically, annoying the hell out of Ortillo. "Enid just landed here; she wasn't staying on the island. I tell you, that Grimaldi woman drowned the girl, set fire to the scientist's cabin, and might kill more campers. One after the other. Attacking one after the other, on a rampage, in case they might have evidence, something they noticed about her. No telling. She may have known both women, maybe invited both of them here to die or just invited one and burned her previous cabin down to hide evidence. That's what they have in common. She might not stop there."

"That's asinine," Deputy Christie said.

"But where the hell *is* she?" Gabriel shouted. "Is *her* corpse going to turn up now?" Head down, he rotated in a half circle, kicking pebbles, scuffing the ground. "Was she the intended victim? Who knew that she had changed cabins—probably only a handful of people, right?" He stood still. "If that many. She moved to 12 at noon when hardly anyone was around. Who was in the Ranger's office when she checked in? Think— who *didn't* know?"

"Ever read Agatha Christie's *Ten Little Indians*?" Adrian asked. "The one who pretended to be a victim was actually the killer."

"Are you OK with this?" Mary asked Spencer. "You hike to the grave-yard while I bike the Quarantine Trail? No trams go to the Pioneer cemetery." She nodded at the trail to their left. "So you'll have to walk both ways from this landing, and then take a tram back to the cabins from here. Can we do this?" She prodded the back tire, testing it. "After lunch, we'll rest and get to the pavilion by 2:00." She unscrewed her water bottle and sipped.

"This is perfect, Mary. Let's face it, you've been dying to get me out of your hair."

"Let's not fight, Spence."

Morgan overheard. He was dragging two kayaks back to the rack, one after the other. He liked Mary, a lot, and wanted her to like him. She was interesting and kind, and reminded him of his Grandmom Miriam. He wished that *she* had come. Pops made him lonely, and he was sick of taking care of the old fart. And the nine-year-old tosser pissed him off, always tagging along. What about next year, when he'd be thirteen? What then? The tosser would only be ten. How could he meet girls with a ten-year-old hanging around?

Waiting by himself at the landing, Sebby noticed the Jiggler sitting at the far end of the dark shelter and hustled to join Morgan. "That guy gives me the creeps," Sebby said.

"Everyone gives you the creeps. You're such a hoser. He's OK."

"Not Gray Man. I don't mean Gray Man!"

"You should write comic books," Morgan told him. "Odd Job? Do you mean Odd Job? Is he here?" He walked away without waiting for Sebby's answer. Morgan had been about to ask Mary if she could use some firewood that night, but she was busy talking with Professor Spencer again: "So, I'll see you back at the cabin. First one back lights the fire."

"Got it." And that was the last thing Spence said to her. The way he saw it, when she nagged, he was free to lie. Exercise, exercise, she always was on his back about exercise. It was none of her business. His wife had been the same way. He had become so good at lying to her, sometimes all truths seemed like falsehoods. It wouldn't even occur to him to tell the truth. He resented having to report to these women, when he stumbled over words and became confused trying to get his story straight. Why couldn't they leave him alone?

As soon as Mary was out of sight, he strolled back to the landing and sat in the shelter, waiting to catch the next tram back to his porch and read. He had no intention of walking to any cemetery. He heard, "Did you see that big wolf dog with those four children? And those two little boys kayaking, all by themselves? They took the boats without paying and without life jackets."

Spence hadn't noticed the large man sitting there in the shade. Startled, feeling a bit guilty, he became unusually loquacious: "Kids. Good heavens. No, I didn't. Imagine that." He filled the silence. "Why, I wouldn't know how to hold a paddle. And I'd get lost. I even have to stop for a minute to remember my way home now, since I moved out of university housing."

"It's tough, getting old. There's no turning back," the stranger stated. "Life isn't easy."

"I can't keep up. And why do I have to? Fighting it is just too much, sometimes." Spence turned away so that he'd see the tram as it approached. He didn't want to miss it.

"It's tough, getting old. There's no turning back," the stranger repeated.

"Life isn't easy," Spence whined. Why was the tram taking so long? "You know, I wish that I *had* done more—fished, biked, years ago. Kayaked at least once. It looks restful, easy. All I wanted here was a little peace and quiet. I'd leave if I could."

"How about leaving in a kayak?" The stranger asked. "Wouldn't that be perfect?"

At that moment and the ones after that, Professor Spencer didn't know quite what to do.

Chapter 10

In the Rangers' Office, Gabriel was confident: "Today, we narrow things down." He turned to Deputy Christie. "Our guy is still here, stuck on an island, surrounded by potential witnesses. Assemble everyone in the pavilion, find out what the campers did during the night, what they saw or heard or scented. We don't have to keep them in the pavilion for long, I think, unless something changes. Let's not test their patience."

He followed the deputies and two rangers out of the office, as far as the top of the stairs. Gazing skyward, he took a deep breath and weighed the challenges. How to monitor two thousand acres and nine miles of shoreline? How to assess fading clues and catch up with departed visitors who were scattering like buckshot? Presuming the murderer was still on the island, how to insure everyone else's safety?

Ranger Edwards remained in his desk chair and swiveled to stare at the white board. So Oscar Coleman got to keep cabin 7 after all, almost as though he had engineered all of this. He squeezed his eyes shut, raised his chin, and shook his head. That would be too crazy.

By 2:20, it seemed to the campers that they had been sitting on their rudimentary benches non-stop, since yesterday. They were somber—those who showed up. Libera, the big Asian, little Sebby, one professor, and several tent campers were among the missing. Some might have gone fishing before the staff told everyone about the interrogation. The assembled campers knew that they wouldn't be going anywhere soon, not with cabin 5's murder attempt. But no one griped, not even the three Colemans. Yet.

Molly Standish took her work seriously, especially that day. She'd do anything to help catch the killer, to renew peace on the island, even though, the past two days, she couldn't wait to return home to her cottage on Block Island. Cayo Costa generally ran like clockwork; the entire crew fulfilled their mission—to share but protect the island. Every spring, her six week stint there just flew by. The rangers were no-nonsense professionals, and unfailingly respectful. At her age, she realized every landscape changes, but Cayo Costa was unique— reverting to its natural state. A hundred years earlier, there was a significant settlement on the island—a trading outpost, a working waterfront, and government facilities. Cayo Costa had been transformed, demodernized and renewed, and she loved it; it gave her hope. All this violence threatened to defile her pure winter retreat.

Monitoring the pavilion, she listened closely to the chatter as Detective Ortillo had asked her to, doing her part. He wanted to know more : campers' backgrounds, their trips to the island earlier in the week, did they know each other previously or recognize someone? She had a unique opportunity to listen, to study people. But she worried that if she took notes, they'd stop talking. Except for Sebby, Spencer, Libera, and Fred Kenichi, the cabin people sat to one side, close to each other. Ranger Edwards and Ortillo asked the staff to concentrate on them rather than the tent folk. Perhaps Libera and Mr. Kenichi were together somewhere, safe, and Morgan insisted that his little brother was on the way. But she worried, imagining that killer somewhere on the island.

"There are two rules of thumb raising children: number one, you cannot treat them differently; number two, you cannot treat them the same," Mary Ellison was telling Phil.

Morgan leaned over. "That's a very trenchant observation, Professor Ellison."

She was, for the moment, speechless.

Bemused, Phil almost blurted that he didn't have to treat the boys any way at all. They were there to have fun.

"Where's Sebby?" Mary asked Morgan, for the second time.

"He couldn't keep up. I ran here."

Mary grimaced and their eyes met.

Boris overheard Ortillo ask Molly if Libera had turned up. He thought that was an unfortunate way of putting it.

"Is Libera the lady who found the body in the kayak yesterday?" he asked Tamara. "And wasn't she staying in the cabin that burned, cabin 5, in front of us? We carried her things from the tram. So who almost died there? Was it her?"

Campers within earshot listened closely, while they observed the three Russian adults pass kielbasa, dried fruit, and a baguette back and forth to each other, eating non-stop. In his harem pants, Boris would have been a show-stopper even without the food and Tamara moved with the grace of a ballerina.

In a corner, Mia Templeton huddled with Roger and the Rodzianko boys: "Stick together, "she hissed. "Follow Wolf. He'll pick up the scent. When we spot the Chinaman again, stick together no matter what, stay hidden, and be quiet. Try not to scream or he might chase you."

"But if we stick together, we can't cover much ground," Roger retorted. "Do you want to break this case, or not?"

"Stick together. Period. That way, Wolf protects all of us."

"How soon before we tell them that Wolf has to go again? I have to too," Stas said.

"Don't say anything, you three just slip out with him when I tie my shoe. That's the signal. Tuck the notebook under your shirt. I'll join you in exactly two minutes. I can tell Mom that you forgot to bring this plastic poop bag if anyone tries to stop me. She gets it. If I don't show up, come back in here. I don't want you guys out there by yourselves."

"You just have to be the boss all the time," Roger whispered. "All the time, always."

"It's my turn to carry the jackknife," Stas said.

During a momentary silence, everyone heard a handsome older woman wearing a pink coral necklace, coral earrings, and a coral pinkie ring tell her husband, "It's a problem, honey. The girls are traveling, and we can't ask our son to pick up the prescriptions. I planned to get your pills yesterday, when we got home."

"Why can't you ask him?" Behind them, the green-eyed woman with the long braid broke in, idly, barely paying attention.

"We don't speak. He's bitter. We're comfortable and he's struggling. What can *we* do about it? How much help is enough?"

"I hear ya," Phil broke in.

"The girls—the complete opposite. Never ever did we favor one child over another. If anything—but the boy seems to despise us. We should have cracked down on him years ago, but we didn't want to treat him differently."

"But enough is enough, right?" her husband offered.

Mary brushed back a soft tangle of white curls and repeated: "There are two iron rules of raising children: one is that you can't treat children differently; the second is that you can't treat them the same."

Mason frowned and stared at her, uncertain where she was coming from. He had brought his own camp chair along, to keep a beverage in the holder, sit back, and relax. It had been a late night and then an early morning, with the fire next door. After the girl was found in the kayak yesterday, he and Will were stuck in the pavilion for hours, right when the fish were running, and here they were again—until who knows when. He was ready to go home. Home looked pretty good right now, especially since that girl Melony kept telling everybody that he had locked her in the bathroom.

He thought that he recognized a middle-aged man with white hair staring ahead, sipping from his water bottle like clockwork. Hadn't that guy walked back to the cabins ahead of them after they all left the pavilion the night before? What cabin could he be in? It was hard to remember, and they couldn't see clearly without a flashlight. And, come to think of it, why did the Asian guy walk ahead of them too? Didn't he belong way back there in cabin 9? Mason grunted, and began to listen to the chatter around him when he heard Will's voice.

"Horses are my weakness," he heard Will tell the Tates. Now, do they know that he means that he has always owned a horse, or do they think he has a gambling problem? Mason wondered. Mason edged closer to the chattering coeds. What were they up to?

One girl was confiding in Waldo. "I'm becoming less of a dwork. Like, I ask questions. Like, about the trust fund, that 'standard procedure' stuff? He always goes, 'it depends' or 'let me worry about that, that's no big deal'. But now I make him explain. You'd be proud of me."

"I would. That's awesome."

Sebby and Morgan were drawing caricatures of the campers surrounding them and bursting into laughter. Phil wondered where the boys had bought the calligraphy kit. Morgan stopped drawing to listen to the coeds. Tiana leaned over to tell the brothers from Maine: "Our first night here, in the site next to us, this fraternity type brings out a machete. A machete! I'm thinking 'This isn't going to end well.'"

Sue, the tallest girl, turned to face Waldo, who was leaning forward. "And the other kids start throwing him oranges and things in the air and he's slicing them with the machete. Then he slices their carton of milk. It was full, too. It went all over the place. And then those kids had no more milk."

The other three nodded, their corn rows bobbing. "We thought that he was showing off for our benefit," Tiana said. "We couldn't get away fast enough. He left yesterday, I guess. Because he's gone."

"Why are there more no-see-ums in the morning and mostly mosquitoes at night?" Rosie whined, examining her calves, not expecting an answer.

Mia tied her shoe and left.

The Nautilus family chatted, mulling over the value of Monday's astronomy program. Tuesday night, they had walked to the beach again, but could only find Orion and then the moon rose. "Hardly any mosquitoes, though," the oldest boy said.

"I have a mental block when it comes to figuring out night skies," his dad said.

Molly resolved to tell the detectives that a family of six had walked from the tents to the beach and back long after dark. They might have seen something. She watched the campers carefully, trying to making sure that no one slipped away but it wasn't easy. The restroom was only fifty yards away, but the last time she stood in the road to make sure someone came back, those children with the dog, and some other camper, had slipped away. But then he might have come back. She wasn't sure.

"You're in social services?" Gilbert asked Keisha. "I admire you. That takes patience. Cayo Costa's just the place to recover from your practice's stress, isn't it?"

"Well, you, know, it's worthwhile work, but a few clients really look at things differently," she answered, thinking that he might be hitting on her but she didn't care. "I have this client in Naples named Cycle—not because everything he owns is piled on his bicycle, but because every time he gets caught stealing, he claims that he found the stuff in a recycle bin. So, actually, a couple weeks ago, *his* bike got stolen. I mean, it was a disaster. I didn't know how he'd cope. But two days later, I see him tooling along on a girl's white and pink bike. 'Where'd you get the bike?' I asked. 'Found it,' the guy told me, dead-serious. 'It was propped up against a garage one morning, unlocked. Four hours later, I went by, it was still there.'"

Boris watched a man at the end of the back row, biting his nails, fidgeting, almost out of Molly's and the Deputy's sight. Possibly the guy was close to erupting, desperate for the case to be solved so that he could relax. Or maybe he had colitis, or maybe he was a fugitive with too many parking tickets. Maybe he knew who did it. The guy looked as if he wanted to shout that if the police would get on the ball, the killer could be apprehended quickly. But maybe the guy was agitated because he was losing precious vacation time, thinking that the police shouldn't be bothering innocent campers, and he wished that someone else would say so.

Was he the only one who noticed this agitated man? Americans don't know what trouble was, he thought. Tamara inherited her mother's apartment during perestroika and became a wealthy woman overnight, but if her stepbrother Paul hadn't sponsored them, the couple would still be back in Tomsk, living next to a river polluted with radioactive material. Lots of Jews and minorities in the professions ended up in Siberia—not as prisoners in the gulag, but because those were the only towns where they could get jobs and apartments and raise their families. Under the Soviets, Jews settled for whatever second-best employment and housing they could get. When he strolled over to look at the shell exhibit across the road, Boris glanced at Sebby's caricatures. They were excellent.

"My boy found the head of a sea turtle in the bushes near the quarantine dock," the Nautilus woman was saying.

"A head?" Phil Schwartz asked.

"You know—the skull. We saw a shell along the shore too, but the tissue was still rotting. Anyway, we're flying back and can't take it with us."

Melony chimed in: "There's a boy, you know, a kid with a backpack who walks around by himself all the time, the one who says he's tracking animals. Maybe he's not staying in his tent. I think that I saw a light in cabin 10 last night, for a minute or two."

Mason interrupted, "That kid—the one that skulks around at night? Where did you see him? Maybe he did the bathroom door. We're talking weird, here."

"We said hello but he didn't even look at us. He may be a deaf mute," Tamara added.

"He isn't." Molly hovered nearby, listening. She didn't know what else to say. She knew who they were talking about, and he *was* different. He lived with his parents and little sister in a private home, as caretakers. When she struggled for words to defend him, she forgot all about the light in cabin 10. Richard drove up; the tram's engine appeared to be smoking.

"Your boss is wanted at the ranger station. I'll give him a lift," he told Deputy Christie.

While they waited for Ortillo to finish talking with Melony and Keisha, Margery asked Richard to chain the rental kayaks under the office building so that no one could use one to leave the island. "The paddles are already locked up in the cage with the lifejackets. Except for two that turned up behind the bike rack. They aren't ours," he said.

"Well, he wants every boat and paddle secured. Those too. We should have done this sooner."

"Right. I'll chain the kayaks and lock those two odd paddles in the cage."

"Perfect."

"What about Libera's and the other private kayaks?"

"Those most of all."

Gabriel's eyes narrowed as they drove reversed near cabin 12, but there was no time to check if she was inside. But why would she still be there? But where *was* she?

Now and then, Libera dismounted and walked the bike over roots or ridges; she managed to skirt deposits of soft sand by riding the rims of the paths with ease. Not only wasn't she sure where she was, but she was surprised when she came upon Quarantine Landing and a placard commemorated the La Costa Station. Was yellow fever still a big problem in 1900? Why else would the US Health Department house a doctor on a walkway one hundred yards offshore, to check every incoming vessel? Yellow fever or malaria seemed logical. Wasn't Dr. Mudd, the Lincoln assassination conspirator, released from exile on the Dry Tortugas because of his exemplary service during a yellow fever epidemic? But wouldn't that have been much earlier?

Bicycling along onto what she thought might be the Scrub Trails, Libera inadvertently circled toward the Dolphin Trail. Then, daydreaming, she turned onto what she thought was, in all probability, the Cemetery Trail. When she spotted a blue bicycle, not a rental, parked on the side of the trail, she accelerated. The bike was unlocked, with two bottles of water in the basket in the front and a rack with a small backpack in the back. She decided to ask the owner for a sip of water, parked her rental, and meandered off the path, looking for someone to ask; after about five minutes, she returned and waited. No one came.

She rode further on and was stunned when the path ended at a dead end, at a low bluff overlooking a beach. She stared at the ocean below.

Where was she? She deserved this dead end, lost on an island that she had visited many times before. Below the bluff, it was low tide, mid-afternoon —later in the day than she thought. In the distance, a solitary jogger ran on the hard-packed sand close to the water, too far away for her to shout and ask him where she was.

It was humid. She was tired, thirsty, discouraged, and disoriented. If only she had taken thirty seconds to glance at the map at the landing before she left, or brought the one in her old shorts. Even using the sun to distinguish east from west, she had no idea where she was. She turned and biked back to the blue bicycle. No one was there. She stopped and listened for voices, confused. If she had taken the wrong turn, she should be downwind from the cabins, but she couldn't smell the smoke from the fire. She retreated and came across a sign for the Scrub Trail, but had no idea which direction to choose. If she was cycling in a circle, shouldn't she have crossed the Cabin Trail that bisected the island? She was so friggin' lost.

Finally, somehow, she came upon the Pioneer Cemetery. She deserved to be in a graveyard, hopeless and helpless, after cycling in circles for hours. She didn't care about the gravesites any more, just as long as she could get back to the landing. Resting the bike against a bench, she sat outside the split rail fence. Her eyes burned with sweat, soot still drifted from her hair, and she'd consider drinking from a wild boar's hole she was so thirsty. Surely someone would come and help.

Only I would be this stupid, she thought. She strolled between the graves, calming down. A graveyard will do that. Those marked by circles of shells probably belonged to small children, to successive wives who didn't survive childbirth, or to seamen who never returned home. Maybe bodies washed up on the shore. As she walked back and forth, studying the inscriptions on the tombstones, she experimented with lyrics to the tune of *Camptown Races* and softly sang:

Peter Nelson lived quite long, do-da, do-da.
From a fitful fever, he passed along, o da do-da day.

Gwine to bike all day,
Gwine to bike all night,
I'm dying of thirst and tired too,
What a way to start the day.

There's a headless statue on Eugene's grave, do-da, do-da,
A lamb or lion made a difference we'd say, O da do-da day.

Francis Coleman wasn't Eugene's son, do-da, do-da,
But Eugene might from Walter have come, o da do-da day.
Lost on Quarantine,
Lost on Scrub Trail too,
I'm dying of thirst and tired too,
I screwed up today.

Stephen Foster never even saw the Suwannee River and probably never went to a Camptown Race either, she mused; and look where that got him. Writing ageless songs in comfort, he had the sense to hang out where it was civilized. She had no idea that he lived in desperation and died an impoverished alcoholic. Feeling as though she were the only one on earth, she sang so that she wouldn't cry.

"Could you please shut up?" A soft voice startled her. "Before Christmas, I found a gopher tortoise right here." At the edge of the woods, not on the path, a tow-headed boy carrying a backpack and walking stick frowned at her. He had a broad face like a cat, accentuated by yellow-green eyes and thin lips.

"I'm lost," she said, peering at the mesh of his backpack, spotting a water bottle. Surely he heard me singing, she thought. He must think I'm strange. Maybe I frighten him.

"Maybe if you didn't make so much noise, you'd pay better attention," he said. "Almost no one gets lost on these trails, especially not here near the cemetery. I live here."

"How do you get to school?"

"Home schooled. I read backwards best. I'm a great fisherman—sheep's head, whiting, pompano," he announced. "Our freezer's full. You missed a couple signs."

"I'm lost. Please. I need water, very much."

He acted as if he hadn't heard—to spare her embarrassment? Libera wondered. Or perhaps he wanted to show off first, or wanted to talk before he helped her? Talking was fine with her, just as long as he gave her water and showed her the way back.

"Last visit, I saw marsh rabbits first thing in the morning," she told him.

"There are armadillos around your new cabin," he confided. "A nine-banded armadillo walked ahead of me there for a long time last month."

"Armadillos? Here?"

"Mostly at night. That's the rustling. Surprise them with your flashlight. You'll see them. They jump around when they're surprised. Didn't you see their prints, Monday, behind your place? I bet that you thought they were raccoon tracks. And do you know what makes those tiny train-track prints on the prairie? Centipedes."

"I'm thirsty," she prompted him. How did this kid know where she had walked on Monday and that she hummed?

"Sorry. Germs."

"Germs?"

"Germs. There'll be water at the landing. You know, before you found the girl in the kayak yesterday, a passenger from Bokeelia landed and just stayed there at the landing."

"How come I didn't see anyone?" Libera asked.

"Too late? Maybe other passengers or someone in the harbor did," he said, nodding once and raising his eyebrows. His eyes were so light, they looked ethereal. Such gravitas in this odd boy, she thought. He can't be more than eight. This is surreal. If I had money with me, I'd pay a fortune for his water. I could die of thirst talking to this little bastard.

"Kayaks came and left while you fished Pelican Bay. If it wasn't that passenger, maybe one of them did it." he said. "A bad guy could have paddled in, attacked, and kayaked right back to Pineland Road, the quick route to the mainland." He chuckled. "As long as the killer kayaked right back. After dark, Tug Henry tows the cars to his garage." He raised his eyebrows. "'Tow Job,' his sign says. 'Best Hookers in Town.'"

Surely he doesn't understand that, Libera thought. "Was anybody hurt in the fire?"

"Died maybe. In your back bunk. Right in your bunk! Maybe somebody thinks it was you," he chortled. "You'd better bring the bike back and pay for it, even though you'd be safer here."

She didn't know what to think, what to believe. Safer? Did someone die? Did this child mean that Gabriel thought that she had died, or that she had set the fire? How did this boy know so much about her—that she hadn't paid, what cabins she slept in? Did he know the killer?

"I'm Libera," she said, and rolled the bike toward him.

"Gregor," he told her. "You say it like that—'grey-gore.'"

"May I have some water, please? Please?"

He shook his head. "No. I already told you that. Here's what you have to do."

Libera was uncertain whether to return the bike or cycle to the cabins. She decided to return the bike first—a fateful decision, as it turned out. Twice, a pavilion full of cabin and tent campers learned that Libera was still alive and being interrogated, but she never saw the group en masse. Except for a few cabin people, she had no idea who else was on the island.

Chapter 11

"Let me in on that dog act, or I'll tell. I know what you're up to."

"So what. We need you like a hole in the head."

"You can't stop me."

"Anyway, the Nautilus boys are joining up so you can't. They know the island. You stick to the college chicks. "

"I saved that woman's life."

"Get lost, pyro," Stas muttered.

Mia ignored both of them and told Roger: "So you guys can slip out, little by little. Meet behind the number 1 shower."

"We're going to get that sucker." Roger nodded and bobbed.

"What if someone takes a shower?" Waldo asked.

"No one will. Not today, not at this time."

The Nautilus boys discreetly slid toward the end of the bench nearest the beach path. Tod was wearing binoculars.

Leaning on the counter in the Rangers' office, Gabriel compared his summary with everyone else's notes. Ranger Edwards looked on: "We still have Fred Kenichi missing—cabin 9, from Fort Myers, arrived Sunday afternoon. Molly says that he did show up after the girl's murder yesterday, a bit late, but didn't show up today. Oddly enough, no one seems to have noticed him except for little Sebby, who said that a 'giant Chinaman' from cabin 9 or 10 left the restroom while he and his brother were horsing around in the shower early this morning. This was while we were putting the fire out. The kid said that he looks like a sumo wrestler in a video game except that this guy's 'really, really old'."

"Everybody looks 'really, really old' to a kid. Doesn't sound like a plausible lead," Adrian said. Neither of the other men had known that he was hovering behind them.

"Look into it," Gabriel told him, not turning around. "He could be our guy. Find him. Five or six of the private homes on the south shore are unoccupied. Go through them with a fine tooth comb. And check the anchored boats in the harbor and the boats at the pier."

"We've already searched the houses and harbor two or three times," Adrian declared. "Wouldn't Kenichi have turned up by now if he's innocent? Should we use force?"

"No. And search again. Everywhere I said." Gabriel added, "Even with the help from the Coast Guard, six counties, and a two dozen police departments, it would take the National Guard to do this right—with all the different ferries, private and rented boats, day cruises, private homes, the campground, and kayaks. Check again." He nodded. "This may be the break we've been looking for. Maybe he killed both of them. And we wouldn't need a much of a motive if we had a madman." He looked at the grisly turtle nest exhibit, the broken shells. "On the other hand, he could be another victim. Check cabin 9 first." He wondered—could a short kid like Sebby be able to see around the shower's partitions? Why didn't the older brother also spot Kenichi?

Annoyed, suspecting that the Chief was assigning him to unnecessary searches, maybe just to get rid of him, Adrian peered at the paperwork. "One murder, one woman critically injured, and one disappearance in 24 hours—and all you can do is hope that it's a madman?" He joggled his head back and forth like a Hawaiian hula doll on a dashboard. "Two disappearances if you include that Grimaldi woman. Can you think of a good reason why she's hiding? But you want it to be the Asian, right? So it's some madman? Not her?"

Gabriel ignored him. The thought of a random killer trapped on the island, killing without compunction, might have sobered him if he wasn't convinced that the crimes were well-planned, in advance. He reviewed his theory with Ranger Edwards, "Hopefully, we'll discover a link between the two women, or between either or both of them with someone on the island. Who knew that they would be here? Enid was on the island for a few minutes; Olivia, a matter of hours. Were they meeting the killer? Those clockwork assaults seem premeditated and executed with precision—the work of a single perp, a patient guy, a thinker."

Adrian chimed in, "Where does the Grimaldi woman come into this? She finds one body, changes cabins, and immediately another woman is nearly burned to death in there. Maybe she spread that accelerant under cabin 5."

"When could she have done it?" Ranger Edwards cut him off. "Someone was with her from 4:30 to 7:00 Tuesday. So she would have had to prepare to burn cabin 5 either before she went kayaking that afternoon or even earlier, before she moved her things to cabin 12 that morning. We drove her back and checked her cabin around 7:00, and shortly after, the campers returned from the pavilion; all her neighbors were milling around there. No one smelled accelerant, ever. Is it feasible that she crawled under cabin 5 in the dark, after bedtime, and did the deed?" He scowled at Adrian. "She told us about the Sterno four-pack, three cans are in still the carton, and a spent one was in yesterday's trash."

Deputy Christie walked in. "The bottled water and sandwiches have arrived."

Adrian persisted. "Why four cans of Sterno? Why four, when she was leaving on Friday, after only a few days?" He paused and grimaced.

"Because she knew that someone was moving into 5 and that it wouldn't be empty. So we can even prove that this was premeditated murder." He leaned on the counter, separating Ortillo and Edwards: "And maybe she *is* a pyro, or even a psycho—jealous of Enid and angry at Olivia for some reason," Adrian said. When he saw the disgusted look on Ortillo's face, he added, "But that would be too complicated."

"Get to work." Gabriel couldn't help shaking his head, scowling. He knew about the cousin's murder back on Grassy Key. Violence did seem to follow Libera around, and he didn't want to mention it. Maybe the killer would turn out to be some madman.

Deputy Christie didn't think Adrian's hypothesis was that crazy, given Libera's behavior and history. It was difficult to believe that she wasn't involved somehow. They should at least learn what made that lady tick. A lot of nutty people live in the Keys, that's why they lived down there.

At that very moment, Gabriel spotted Libera, wheeling the bike to the shed. "Where the hell have you been?" he shouted. "There was a fire!" He stomped toward her, waving his arms.

"Where was I supposed to be?" she replied calmly. "The bucket brigade seemed to have things in hand. I would have been in the way."

"We didn't know if you were dead or alive," Deputy Christie added coldly. "And another camper has disappeared. Can you tell us anything about the Oriental man in cabin 9? He may look like Goldfinger's Odd Job—from the James Bond movie? Have you seen him today?"

Libera shook her head but didn't say a word. Fred? Odd Job? Ortillo waited, studying her. She looked deep in thought, poignant, sweaty, and simply splendid. If only we were here under different circumstances, Gabriel thought. It would be such a pleasure to get to know her—this refined but eccentric, tough but heart-stopping woman. We're the same age. Imagine! Am I crazy, or is something going on here? And as tired and bewildered as she was, willing all this awful business to pass, even though Fred was on her mind, Libera stared at Ortillo longer than the occasion warranted—how magnificent he was, how able, how sweet.

Shortly after 2:00, when almost all the campers were assembled in the pavilion, Mary Ellison stormed up to Deputy Christie: "Something has happened to Spencer. Otherwise, he would have lit the fire. He'd be here. This CSI stuff is the only thing that interests him besides his books."

Before Deputy Christie could say a word, confused, thinking that Mary might be referring to the fire at cabin 5, Mary wailed, "Listen to me. You have to find Spence. Are the boys here?"

Deputy Christie tried to calm her: "Where and when did you last see the professor?" but stopped abruptly and waved to Ranger Edwards. "Would you take over here, please? Mary Ellison and I have to go back to the landing to talk to Detective Ortillo for a moment." She motioned to Mary to climb into the Jeep, executed a three-point turn and headed back toward the Rangers' office just as Gabriel was bounding down the stairs.

"Not now, Deputy Christie. Not now, OK?"

"But it's the professor. He's missing."

"Not now," he muttered.

"What if he had a heart attack somewhere, Chief?"

"Then we'll find him, in the course of ongoing searches." He looked over his shoulder. "Would someone please drive Professor Ellison back to her cabin?"

"Spence's book is still there," Mary shrieked. "At the cabin. If he had come back, he would have *Boat Goat* with him. He was annoyed that I made him leave it; he was dying to finish it. But he needed exercise."

Less than an hour later, Professor Spencer turned up. Way up.

"What the hell with these kayaks." Gabriel cried. "How in hell did a body get up on the top rack?" And then he answered his own question. "The only way to do it was to take a kayak down, put the corpse in, and slide it up, tipping it up about three feet, tier by tier, right to the top. The murderer had to be tall, but not necessarily a weightlifter." A madman, a psychopath maybe, he thought.

Deputy Christie said, "Good thing that Richard went to chain the kayaks. What if that body had stayed up there in this heat?"

Adrian overheard. "I'll tell you who's going to be staying here in the heat. Us! Two murders in kayaks and the arson. Maybe she stuck him up there so we'd think that she couldn't have done it at her age. What will the lady pull next?" He didn't realize that Libera was leaning against a bicycle, just a few feet away.

"Let's stop wailing about 'what next?' and figure out who did it," Libera said, approaching the group. "Please bring me back to my cabin. I need rest, food, and a shower. Then I want to help. Was that poor man strangled?"

Adrian's eyes widened. The nerve of the bitch!

"We think so. Let me take you back, Libera," Gabriel said. "I want to talk, and be sure everything's all right before you go in." Now, in the midst of all this, he realized that he wanted to spend as much time with her as possible. It was crazy, totally unlike him. What was he thinking? There was no denying that it tickled him that they were so at ease with each other and maybe on the same wave length, no longer alone, not at all. But wasn't he mad to even imagine a romance—with one, two, or possibly three killers on the loose? The heart has reasons that reason knows not of.

He paused and turned to Edwards and the deputies. "Look, no one can get off the island—we'll catch this guy, today, maybe tomorrow. We have to."

"Because we can't keep feeding all these people," Adrian blurted. "And Chief—two murders in three days and arson with intent to kill—wait 'til the Commissioner and the press learn about this! And more campers are missing. And we need paper products right away!"

"Look, we'll handle this. The whole department, the rangers, the Coast Guard, police forces across the state, and the feds are helping. And the staff knows the terrain better than I know my back yard."

"You don't have a backyard anymore, Chief. Not since the divorce."

"Tell me about it."

"Olivia," Deputy Christie stated, scanning the campers in the pavilion. "Olivia Longo. Originally from Rhode Island, a renowned research scientist, a geneticist, moved to Gainesville, then Sanibel. Did anyone know her?"

Keisha piped up from the front bench: "We only met her yesterday when she arrived, before anyone heard about the murder. Melony and I were surprised that she only brought two backpacks and a cooler, less than some day trippers."

"That's why there wasn't anything on the table or the porch, probably," Melony added. "She didn't bring gear, didn't cook, and didn't light a fire. If she packed sandwiches and water that would be enough."

"And maybe just a Danish or health bar for breakfast," Keisha added. "She seemed like a super lady. Ran marathons, she said, planned to stay four nights, came here as a kid." She pursed her lips and paused. "You should talk to those yahoos in cabin 6, the ones locking ladies in the toilet." Christie knew that she was just trying to help.

The other campers just listened, stared, and shook their heads, expecting to be released from the pavilion momentarily. Since the fire, though, the danger seemed more diffuse and imminent, random yet real, and they had mixed feelings about wandering freely around the island—even in groups. How could they forget the brutal arson, even for a minute? The burnt smell would last for days, possibly weeks. They couldn't wait to get upwind to the tents, the trails, or the beach. And then, when Ortillo arrived, they learned about Spence.

Within minutes after that, Ranger Hernandez raced up and leapt out of his jeep, within two feet of the pavilion. He trotted up to Gabriel. "We had a call. The man in cabin 8, Gilbert Newsome, belongs to the same kayak club in Cape Coral as Enid Sommers. And their president said that the two had become 'pretty cozy'." Everyone turned and looked at Gilbert.

"Gilbert Newsome?" Gabriel shouted.

Gilbert stood. "There's something I should tell you."

When the Lee County Sheriff's car pulled into the driveway, Claudia came to the door. "Gil did it, the bastard," she began.

She took one look at their faces, shrugged, and threw her head back. "I was so pissed," she spat. "I only wanted to scare the little brat. When she didn't fight, I couldn't figure out what was going on—her not moving. Then it was too late. I thought she was just holding her breathe, so I hung on. How would I know?" She waited, annoyed that the officers didn't say a thing. "I took the Tropical Star over, did the deed—it was too easy. Like I said, what did I know? She should have struggled. What was that about? Not my fault. It was too easy."

She stepped back. "Afterwards, I stole a rental kayak at the landing and paddled back to Jug Creek—didn't you notice that a kayak was missing? It's floating out there. Finders keepers. I had to use the brat's paddle—it's a Werner, nice. Take it. It's in the garage." She closed the door a bit. "Let me just tell the maid to take the Yorkie home with her."

"We'll take care of that, Ma'am."

She hesitated. A gun was inside the side table in the vestibule, right next to her, but she decided that she wanted to live. She knew an excellent lawyer.

Chapter 12

After Ortillo dropped her off and they chatted, Libera fell into a sound sleep. When she woke, it was dark. Why had she not taken a shower when she had the chance? And now, as tired as she was, she had to pee. She couldn't remember where she had tossed the key. She had to go.

Gabriel Ortillo slept in cabin 3 near the washroom furthest away from her, too far.

She headed for the facility next door to her cabin and marveled at the clarity of the scrub in patches of moonlight. Why turn the flashlight on? Even if she closed her eyes, her feet could find the sandy path. But even with her eyes open, she didn't notice a lone figure slip around the corner and into the shower stall.

She remembered that the Ladies Room was on the right in that facility, left the door open, and placed the flashlight on the sink. Moonlight poured through the skylight and clerestories. There was tissue, but no paper towels, so she used her nightie to wipe her hands. Campers raided the towels regularly—for kindling, napkins, and toweling.

But how could the wind have blown the door shut on such a still night? She pushed the door and felt resistance. The crude wooden block had obviously rotated and locked it. Perhaps Melony loosened the nail when she battered the door open and gave Mason hell, because Libera easily booted it open. She lit the flashlight, located the burst lock, and placed it under the sink for the staff to find.

Stunned when the door burst open, the stalker scampered away from the light beam, slipped into the shower stall again, and froze. Libera stood on the top step and scanned the area, wide awake, uneasy. Then she turned to walk back to her cabin and paused. A thin stream of clouds drifted back and forth over the moon; patches of light flickered and disappeared.

Behind her, to her right, she heard rustling. An alarmed bird twittered. Was she going to see an armadillo at last? Was Gregor right? She whirled around and moved toward the sound. The man slid away from the beam and flattened himself against the other side of the shower, confused, wondering what she was doing, wondering if she sensed that he was there. Could she hear him, smell him, read his mind? He froze.

The rustling ceased. She directed the light back and forth across the spot where she had heard movement, holding steady, waiting. She stayed still, taking her time, hoping that the animal would move again.

After a few moments, she turned back to the dark path, but stood still, listening. She decided to take another look at the broken lock, so she swiveled back toward the restrooms. And saw that a big man loomed close behind her. He didn't move, stunned. She shone the light in his face and moved forward. "What are you doing here?" she demanded.

He cajoled her: "You're not well, my dear. I heard about the dead girl in the kayak."

She kept the light on his face, confused. Was she dreaming? What did he mean? "What are you talking about? How did you *get* here? Are you staying in a tent?" Even in the faint light, she could see his bespectacled, protuberant eyes and the downturned mouth above her. Why did he look so different tonight?

"I kept your secrets, Sweetheart. But they're going to find out. This has to stop." He moved closer. "Before you kill again. You won't be able to bear it when they put you away. That's what happens."

He had a rope in his hands. "We don't want that. Not for you."

"Kill *again*?" she asked. "Don't be ridiculous."

"Don't you remember? Maybe you can't. You might not realize what you're doing. They'll destroy you. I can't let that happen."

He lifted the rope. "I wanted flames and ashes—your ashes drifting into the sea, like your plans for Nita, a blessing and a sacrifice. That would have been nice. But this is the best we can do, now."

"What have you done? Oh my God, what have you done?" she asked. "Did you burn that poor woman?" Furious, she slapped him, pulled him forward, and stomped on his right instep with her wrong foot, the sea urchin foot. She grabbed his shirt, preventing him from falling backward, and then dropped him, losing her grip on the flashlight. As she stepped back and kicked it, it rocketed away, the beams rolling across the leaves as it plunged into the brush.

And then, without the light, she became afraid.

"Get away from me!" She scrambled away and around him as he paused, confused, on his hands and knees. She imagined how many strides it would take to reach Gabriel's cabin. Too many. This guy could probably run like a deer. He used to play basketball.

"I can't, Libera," he groaned, getting to his feet, holding the rope taut in front of him. "Don't let's fight, Sweetheart. I can't bear to fight with you."

She bent forward, posing, pretend to listen. She mentally reviewed what she had to do next —so that she could run.

She seized the middle of the rope and pulled him close so that she could wrap her right leg around his left, and pushed him to the ground.

Then she dashed toward cabin 11, next door. She was astonished that she couldn't run faster. In fact, she seemed to be slowing down, barely loping. Had the Russians left? She had no idea since she wasn't interrogated with everyone at the pavilion.

She scooted down the road to 10. The porch was swept clean and no embers burned in the fire ring; the site looked empty. And so did cabin 9, but she cowered next to the porch for a moment, listening. It was quiet and seemed deserted. She didn't dare go up onto the unscreened porch and knock. Clouds no longer covered the moon. Bounce would see her.

And could he hear her? Where was he? Once he was on his feet, he'd search for her. Everything was quieter than her breathing. He could be close by, watching and waiting. She couldn't stay there. Every single breathe, even her nightie fluttering, might be noticed in the still, bright night. Bent over, she dashed across the road and crawled from bush to bush, past cabin 4.

"Where are you, dear?" he called softly. On his knees, bent over, searching for his eyeglasses, his hands swept back and forth in half circles. Trembling, he couldn't stand until he found them. How would he find her if he stepped on them? What would he do then?

Finally, he rose, brushed the sand off, and put them on. "Where are you?" he whispered again, leaning forward, listening. Squinting into the brush on either side of the path, he walked slowly past the shower stall where he had been lurking and peered into the cubicles. Moonlight wafted through the trees. She had fled. He had to find her.

"I can help," he mouthed, barely speaking. "Come here, sweetie." He walked a few steps, scanning the underbrush along the moon-flecked path. "Come on now."

Libera crouched next to the charred ruins of cabin 5, waiting for clouds to drift across the moon. It was quiet. Somewhere, that huge man was

listening, hunting her. Then, she heard him sing, slowly, in an eerie fal-
setto: "Sleepy time gal, when all your dancing is through. Sleepy time gal,
I'll find a cottage for you." What the hell! Dad's lyrics! How did he know?
How could he?

Cramped, afraid that she might topple over, worried that she'd be too
stiff to run, she shifted her weight. Beneath her, a board snapped.

He pounded past her, not five feet away, running at top speed on the
speckled moonlit path. Taking a deep breath, she bolted to her right, to the
porch steps of cabin 4, and huddled.

Where was he? How far away, on which side of her? Why hadn't she
listened, paid attention to how far he ran? Could he have gone away, afraid
that someone might have heard them? Thin clouds drifted across the moon.

Libera tiptoed with huge steps to cabin 6 and dropped to her knees in
the middle of the sea grapes against the wall. A bird trilled in alarm, once.
Squatting under the shadow of a propped-up shutter, she tried to hold still,
gripping her knees, quaking. It was quiet. She wanted to cry. How could
this be happening? It was absurd. She imagined losing control and laughing, being unable to stop laughing, at the thought of crouching there like
that until daylight. She feared the exhaustion, the absurdity, the danger,
if she actually fell asleep there. But if he couldn't find her, surely he would
go away. Maybe he already had. She was so tired.

Then she heard him walking toward her, slowly walking. Walking,
hesitating, and walking. "The girl in the kayak, dear? The police will be
all over this island, searching for you." That was all he said. She waited.
Had he left?

Cowering, her cheek against the wall, she strained to see her cabin
through the trees. Could she make it there? But what if he were there,
waiting for her? He might go inside and wait for her. Could he have
walked there without her hearing him?

What if he was nearby? What if he knew where she was, right now, all along, and he was watching?

"I'm waiting, dear."

Was he closer? She didn't dare lift her head. Out of the corner of her eye, she spotted Will's short metal shovel a few feet away, resting against the porch steps, next to his fishing rods, but she didn't dare inch toward it.

"They'll put you away. You won't be able to bear it." She heard shuffling. Was he inching toward the sound of her thudding heart?

"Come here, sleepy-time gal. Come on now." Had he become accustomed to the dark, looking in her direction, able to see shapes? Was he holding that rope?

She tried not to shake. The clouds drifted away from the moon. She ducked. Could he sense motion, trembling? She heard rustling.

"Libera?" a voice asked, over her shoulder. "What's up, Babe?"

She froze. "I'm outside your window," she whispered.

"This, I know. Bartenders' ears, Baby, bartenders' ears," Will whispered back. Not four inches from her face, he asked, "Why are we whispering? What's up? There's a little Scotch left."

"A man is trying to kill me," Libera sobbed. "He's following me and there's a full moon."

This is so crazy, she thought—like a confessional. "He's singing a song my father used to sing. He must have heard me humming the tune on Grassy Key. It's the same guy!"

"No shit! You come on in here. Ignore Mason. He snores like a band saw."

"Be quiet," she whispered.

She slid to the front of the cabin, crouched beside the steps, and was surprised when Mason emerged first, still in his bathing suit. "Some fella chasing you? You come sit with me," he said, put his arm around her shoulders, and helped her slide up to the top step. "Let's see if we can turn off Will's boyish charm for a minute or two," he said, and sighed. "This is serious business."

Will jumped off the side of the porch and joined them, sitting on the bottom step. He kissed Libera, first on one knee, then on the other, and said: "Nothing we can't handle, Libby darling. Nothing we can't handle. Need a paper towel? We got lots. Damned shame we got a cabin without a screened porch. We'd be cozy if it weren't for the mosquitoes. You missed some fine fishing tonight. We waited."

"Do you have a whistle?" she asked. Mine is fastened to the life vest." Neither man said anything, savoring the situation. She scooted down, next to Will.

"Is SOS three short, three long, three short, or is it three long, three short, three long?" she asked. She thought for a moment that he didn't hear her.

After a silence, he replied. "Three long, three short, three long."

Mason asked, "What's the plan?"

"Get help. What else?" Will asked. "Wake up the detectives."

He nodded toward his cabin. "Messy in there, but you could lock yourself in. Ortillo moved into cabin 3, right?"

"I'll stay out here with Mason," she said. "You two are great."

"If you only knew," Will answered.

Chapter 13

"She resisted, God bless her, and then those guys in cabin 6 came out and he ran away." Gabriel waved his arms at Margery and Adrian. "And we now know that he's definitely the guy who burned cabin 5 the night before, thinking that she was in there—like some ritual sacrifice. We have to nab him."

"So she says. She's still a prime suspect—for both the professor's murder and the arson," Adrian insisted, jutting out his lower lip.

"Get outa here. Mrs. Newsome's in custody—you were dead wrong there, and this Bounce guy told Libera that he set the fire."

"That's her story."

"Her story makes sense. What about Gregor's encounter with her in the cemetery, when she got lost?" Margery asked.

"That's no alibi, so long after the fire." Adrian added, "Now if the kid actually saw this Grassy Key maniac stalking her—that would be helpful. No one can corroborate her story. Trust me."

"Why? But we have to consider that even if we had more than one killer, are we missing something?" Gabriel muttered.

"That she might be part of a conspiracy, involved in one, maybe more? No one has found the kids, right?"

"Get a life, Fitzhugh." Gabriel walked away.

"He doesn't want to hear it," Adrian mumbled to Margery. "Ortillo's gaga about her, on a first-name basis. Calls her 'Libera', by her first name."

She shrugged, but he was on a tear: "And what about the dead cousin in the Keys last fall?"

"Give me a break. How is that relevant?" Margery looked over the roster. "Our man is Bruce Brueghel, tent site 30. And there's no way he'll get off this island."

Late Thursday afternoon, Spence's body was transported to the mainland. Mary accompanied the remains, surprised that she wasn't grieving more. She wished that she had had a chance to talk with Morgan and Sebby before she left, to tell them to be more careful.

Libera told Ortillo everything that she knew about Bounce, and she was surprised that it wasn't much, even though they had been neighbors for years. Her bruises from the attack had turned purple-grey. Ortillo had to fight the impulse to take her in his arms. After Libera discussed Bounce, trying to think where he might hide, she also recalled what they both had overlooked when they discovered Enid—a paddle should have been in or near the Squall, unless Enid had climbed out and carried it somewhere. No killer would have left it floating at the scene, attracting attention. "I should have noticed," she said out loud. "How could I have missed that? Whoever removed the paddle probably needed it, to kayak back to the mainland. You could have caught her right away."

"It would have helped us," he said. "To realize that there were two killers. I'll never know why we discounted this so soon. But we can't figure out why two pricey paddles turned up behind the boat rack," he mused. "Richard says that they weren't there the day before."

After a pause, Libera said that she planned to take the morning ferry back to Bokeelia, if she wasn't needed anymore. Gabriel wished that she wasn't leaving, and he searched for a way to ask her to wait for him to finish the case. He wished that they could walk to the beach and wait for the sunset together like all the other couples, but he had to get back to work. He was trying to think of some way to say that, when they noticed a large figure plodding toward them along the southwest dunes through the deep sand, framed by the glare, followed by a cluster of children and a large dog. That broad silhouette could only be Fred Kenichi.

"A man needs help," he began, as soon as he was within earshot. "I propped him up behind the old house with the dock near the manatees." He waited, surprised that neither one said anything. Out of the corner of his eye, Fred watched the children scamper away, dragging Wolf, who appeared to want to stay behind.

"I'd been meditating there. The children show up now and then, hiding in the trees. They've been doing this. I didn't mind. Then, for some reason, this fellow crept up behind them and started asking weird questions, frightening them, and yelling at the dog to stop his barking. So the kids start screaming, the dog goes crazy, bites him, and I had to get a little rough with him. Not the dog—the crazy fellow who needs help. No bleeding, but probably internal injuries. I can explain."

"Can a vehicle get in there?" Gabriel turned and asked Ranger Edwards.

"I can explain," Fred repeated palms up, with Gabriel's back to him. "He came at me. I was a black belt, back in the day. Am I in trouble?"

What a beautiful, solid man, Libera thought. How she had missed him, hoping for just a glimpse of him. She wanted to fold into his solid presence, his solemnity, the soft voice, and respectful mean. She would never forget how he bent to suck her foot—so naturally, so authentic, so caring. She had never met anyone like him.

"Don't worry about it," Gabriel said abruptly, turning, already on his way, not wanting to waste time on Kenichi—the madman he once was looking for.

Fred was dumfounded. Libera moved closer to him, watching the sun begin to set, and finally asked, "Are you alright?"

He nodded. They turned to watch the descending sun. After a moment, he snorted and then guffawed. "More than alright. Maybe I shouldn't be telling you this—I feel better than I've felt in years. Sometimes tissue remembrance recreates old skills that are such a joy. If I tell you how much I enjoyed beating the stuffing out of that poor man, would that make sense?"

"Perfect sense. I would have loved to have seen it," she said. "It would make *me* feel better than I have in years. I only wish that I had been there. Let's go watch the sun set."

He took her hand. "Would you me to give you a blow-by-blow description?"

"Please do." She laughed a huge belly laugh. Then she stopped and lowered her head, still and silent, peace flooding in and around her. He waited. And she raised her face to his and whispered, "Let's both feel better than we have in years."

Walking in the opposite direction, Gabriel looked back over his shoulder, spotted the couple, and whirled around. He stood, watching them, rooted to the spot. Were their heads were together, how close together? Then he saw Fred's arm slide around Libera's shoulders. Framed by a glorious sky, the couple leaned into each other. What the hell! Gabriel thought. Why had he left him there with her? Why? Couldn't he have at least told her, "Catch you later?" Because he intended to. He definitely did. They should have questioned Kenichi and kept him away from her. What the hell! What a fool he was!

Fred and Libera chatted and watched the sun until there was only a thin line of light on the horizon and then headed back to the cabins, suffused with happiness.

"It's a miracle that we met this week on this island, detained here together," she said. "What made you leave your quiet life and come here?"

"The Greeks," he replied, stopping, turning toward her.

"I know it's forward of me—but could we keep in touch?" She leaned toward him.

"Sounds like a plan," he replied. He couldn't stop smiling.

An Advanced Peek:

Poppy Tears
A Victorian Mystery

Chapter 1

London, 1872

"Three babies. Dead." Lyon Playfair, standing member of the House of Commons for Edinburgh and St. Andrews, shuffled around the Coroner's Office, fingering the dissecting tools. The smell of formaldehyde was so strong, he could taste it. "Does not this case warrant attention, George? Three? In one family?" His black boots squeaked on the damp white tiles, tracking mud across the floor.

"God's grief, Lyon. If I took myself from house to house checking on dead children, this office wouldn't have time to investigate serious crimes." George Platt, a burly bespectacled man wearing a floor-length apron, replaced two scalpels in the cabinet and didn't turn around. "One hundred and fifty dead babies were found in the Thames and in the street these past twelve months. In the streets! As your Health of Towns Committee is very well aware."

"And that is treated as a sanitation problem, Platt—not criminal."

"Quite. I grant you that infant deaths are excessive. Among the improvident classes," he added. "Children of the poor are by nature fragile. Nature weeds them out, strengths the race. Providentially. Where would we be if Nature didn't?"

"Healthier," Playfair answered. He frowned, studying the way Platt's curious red hair, unfashionably short, stood on end, and stated, "Truth be told, many infant deaths in the city must be by human hand—through want, negligence, or worse. Else, Nature equips babies of every class to survive."

"Bah!" Platt locked the cabinet and studied Playfair. "You've been listening to that charlatan Fortescue."

"Not a bit. When Father served as Inspector General of Hospitals in India, it was clear that poor children perished due to deplorable living conditions, while babies from comfortable families survived. The disparity was marked. Living hand to mouth, families who could not support excess children roundly neglected and abandoned them—or did them in, with impunity, in great numbers."

"Gads. Surely, you're not comparing those barbarians with our race, Playfair." Lyon didn't answer. He was trying, without success, to recall the face of his beloved Indian ayah, the bright and lovely woman who had raised him until he was six. What had become of her? He longed for comfort, for his wife.

George picked up a mallet and then a hacksaw. "Infant death—Nature weeds them out. Darwin. Natural selection. No question."

"But you *did* investigate the death of one child recently—a baronet," Lyon said softly. "At a baby farm."

"By Jove, it was awful. Slept to death, my dear. Fed opium until he convulsed. And he was the heir. The nurse will hang for it."

"It's a wonder that you ascertained the cause of death. 'Slept to death,' you wrote. Interesting."

"What do you infer, Sir?"

"Need I elaborate, Platt? England consumes so much opium—as a stimulant, an intoxicant, a medication, a food, and a sedative—it's difficult to determine whether death results from medical problems, excess excitement, or the sedative Mother's Helper." Playfair pulled out his pipe, hesitated, and put it back in his pocket. "Perchance facilitated by pernicious intent. Especially when a baby dies."

George turned around and stepped forward. "Opium is a precious gift. Indispensable. In the home, on the street, on the battlefield, the Empire thrives on opium, Lyon. Every physician recommends it. Not a kitchen without it." His chin jutted forward. "Playfair, you're casting aspersions on this office. As a gentleman and a scholar, this is unworthy of you."

"Three dead babies," Playfair said.

"I challenge you, Sir. Prove it. Prove that those infant deaths were out of the ordinary and worthy of investigation. Prove it, Sir."

90442584R00086

Made in the USA
Columbia, SC
04 March 2018